"You're riding on my train. And you ain't paid up!"

X-ooming FDR 1932   *Frontispiece (Page26)*

Time Travel Twins

X-ooming FDR
1932

W. Green

ZIPPY BOOKS®

VELOCITER - SECURUS - ERUDITIO

Time Travel Twins: X-ooming FDR 1932 by W. Green
Copyright © 2013, 2022 William R. Green.
All rights reserved
.
Published by Zippy Books
822-928-406- ZippyBooks.com

Frontispiece Illustration by Davide Vaz Raimondi

ISBN-13: 978-0615867717 (Zippy Books)
ISBN-10:0615867715

TIME TRAVEL TWINS

By W. Green

Saving JFK
X-ooming FDR – 1932
X-ooming FDR – 1933
X-ooming FDR – 1934
Saving Trump

Zippy Books

"*The first step in liquidating a people is to erase its memory. Destroy its books, its culture, its history, Then have somebody write new books, manufacture a new culture, invent a new history. Before long, the nation will begin to forget what it is and what it was. The world around it will forget even faster...The struggle of man against power is the struggle of memory against forgetting.*"   -Milan Kundera-

CONTENTS

-1932-

-Introduction-

-Introduction- On June 26, 2028, Zak Newman, an adventurous seventeen-year-old, created his first time-travel log entry. He described the miseries of life in America in 2028 under the dominion and control of the repressive government known disparagingly as "MOM." As chronicled in *Saving JFK*, he and his friends, twin brother and sister Ethan and Emma Callan-Wright, and inventor Dr. A.C. Currant, first used the *TimeTravelle* time machine to enter the world of 1963, attempting to save the life of President John F. Kennedy.

From Zak's diary:

"I can't say enough bad things about MOM. She has location-revealing nano-implants delivered into the bloodstreams of unsuspecting children when they are immunized against disease; mind-control devices that continuously force-feed mental poison into the masses; monitoring cameras and microphones in every inch of public space; police armed with sound detectors able to listen in on private conversations from a half-kilometer distance; and sensing devices in every police cruiser that can identify every license plate number, every occupant, and anything and everything in a person's vehicle.

MOM is like a nasty, nosy dog with bad breath — totally invasive, always in your face, everywhere and nowhere, sniffing about without reason — just an annoying pest that will never leave you alone. She always claims to be working in everyone's best interest, offering the comfort of security and protection, but nobody wants her, and nobody likes her — she's just a bitch. I've been told that many years ago, people and politicians actually discussed the limits of MOM. Many suggested that the government's real job is to maintain the free flow of ideas and accomplishments by protecting the people from outsiders or insiders who might interfere with the 'American Dream,' as it was then called. But after a while, MOM poked her snoopy wet nose into everybody's life, according to her, to help 'them' because 'they' could not possibly help themselves. She became nosier and nosier. She kept improving her hunting dog senses and memory until people now believe that she can identify any individual harboring any unwanted thought anywhere on the planet. Even if this is not true, the people are timid and fearful. This long-distance mind-reading could be just a wild rumor, but I notice more people humming to themselves as they walk about in public. Maybe they're trying to stifle their thoughts. After all, if you don't have an opinion, there's nothing for MOM to read.

As A.C. Currant, the inventor of the TimeTravelle proclaimed boldly from the safety of his underground bunker: 'Screw MOM!' And I'll second that motion. It's time to do something about her. It's time to fix things."

Now the time-traveling twins and Zak are twenty-one years old. They remain steadfast in their goal to improve their world by changing the past. The year is 2032. Life has not improved in the four years following their last time-travel adventure. Their world remains a cocoon of ignorance caught in a web of fear. Spying drones fill the sky, from giant triangular flying platforms to insect-sized bugs. All conversations, human interaction, and even personal thoughts could be monitored. However, no one in their east coast hometown of Mystic Heights knows for sure because the outside world's reality is unknown. Citizens do not speculate. They do not congregate; they do not complain; they do not have opinions. And they never attempt to venture into the unknown. It's too dangerous. People often disappear in the middle of the night. It's a prison world filled with entertaining government-approved distractions designed to keep the minds of the masses occupied and confused. However, escape is possible for some who have a time machine like Dr. Currant's *TimeTravelle*.

Most people in the year 2032 view time travel as science fiction. Zak, Emma, and Ethan know better. It's real. They've done it. Now, despite all the risks, including capture by MOM's time cops, they want to do it again. They have set the date on the time machine to July 13, 1932, and they are ready to travel one hundred years back to another world to exhume the life and legacy of an unknown, historically obscure politician: Franklin Delano Roosevelt.

-Chapter I-

They're Gone!

"Well, don't blame me. I didn't hijack the *TimeTravelle*. You're responsible for your adventurous munchkins, Warren...not me." Dr. A.C. Currant temporarily ended the battle of words waged in Warren Wright's private study and safe room. Along with Jacques Dufour, the two men sat around a small, finely crafted oak table, a gift from one of Wright's clients from his private detective days. Currant downed the last of his drink and slammed the glass onto the table. The empty glass that once held his favorite Johnnie Walker Black Scotch whisky was all that remained of a more civilized conversation that began a half-hour earlier.

"They're just kids," said Warren Wright.

"Hey. They're twenty-one. What were you doing when you were that age?" asked A.C. Currant.

Wright thought it over. "Me. I was in the Army. M.P. Breaking up bar fights."

"That's right. They're not kids anymore."

"Easy for you to say. You don't have any children," said Wright. "I'm not worried about the boys. They can take care of themselves. But I worry about Emma. She's young, pretty, and inexperienced in the ways of the world. She's an easy target. And from what I've read, 1932 is a pretty rough place." He rested his elbow on the arm of the chair and ran his thumb and forefinger over his mustache. His mind drifted away as he held a gently clenched fist to his chin.

"Yes...I have been blessed. No kids." Currant nodded and smirked. Then he glanced back at Wright, who looked pained. "Of course, I'm like an uncle to Emma and Ethan. And even that rascal Zak. They all love me, Warren."

"Humph," said Wright, his focus returning to the

physicist, "Uncle A.C." He shook his head. "That would mean you, and I would be related. I'm not buying that."

Jacques Dufour, a man of delicate sensibilities, was unsettled by the combative conversation. Waiting for a break in the action and sitting between the two hardheaded Yankees, he stroked his goatee with one hand and gently ran his fingertips over the table's inlaid wood designs. He wished he could escape the heat of the discussion, but he was there for a reason. These two needed a referee. Warren Wright was wildly disturbed about the situation, and A.C. Currant was...well...A.C. Currant.

From years of personal experience, he was a man Dufour knew to be a total pain in the royal *derriere*. Push him too hard, Mr. Wright, and you will get a face full of verbal feces. *Mais oui.* I must persevere, he thought, wishing he was somewhere else. "All right, gentlemen. Let's keep it respectful. Nobody asked for this. Nobody is blaming you, Doctor. And, Warren, I think it is clear now that the Twins and Zak were operating independently. Somehow, without the help of Dr. Currant, they gained an understanding of the workings of his invention, and they escaped this world. Let us face facts. Number one, they are adults. They are responsible for their actions. And number two, they are gone. They may not be back for twenty-eight days. Lastly, we can do nothing to alter these facts."

"Are you kidding, Dufour? They may never return. Saving Roosevelt. My ass. Who will be next? Abe Lincoln? They don't know what they're dealing with. They don't understand my time machine. They..."

Warren Wright interrupted Currant's verbal diarrhea. "Jacques, you're the history professor. Tell us what they're up to. Maybe we can develop our own plan if we understand their game plan."

Dufour cleared his throat and glanced back and forth at the two men before speaking. "Your children are good students of history, Warren. We first discussed this topic in their senior history class a few years ago. I am, unfortunately, to blame again. Emma, Ethan, and Zak were, shall we say, disappointed with the aftermath of their time travel to save Mr. Kennedy four years ago. Obviously, the good man still died. And although the impact of that flight provoked controversy about the JFK assassination that still smolders in some circles today, it didn't change the basic nature of our world here in 2032. We still have our super-repressive, controlling, and invasive government." He looked around as if someone might be listening.

"Relax, Jacques," said Wright. "This room is totally isolated."

"Right," said Dufour, reminding himself that this was one place where he was free to say anything without fear of repercussions. "Sadly, the Twins and Zak wanted to do more. They were looking for the key to open the door of freedom for all.

"You mean they're still hoping to eliminate our great white mother…MOM?"

"Err…maybe not so much eliminate, Warren. But I think they would like to balance the forces of government supervision and individual freedom. They are not looking for a political revolution. They know MOM is too powerful to be changed by the life or death of one man as President of the United States. MOM is our secular religion. MOM has her history, hierarchy, dogma, and rituals. She also has her armies, secret police, oppressive surveillance, and prisons. She has a total recall of our every movement, thought, and action. Practically speaking, we are all believers, or we become heathens." He shook his head. "And heathens, as we know, are often burned at the stake."

"So what possessed them to hijack my time machine?" asked Dr. Currant. "More of your wild academic speculation?"

"Call it what you like. They are looking for political evolution. Such evolution might be possible. Little changes here and there in history might shape the future in a positive direction. Our life here in 2032 might change.

I don't think anyone would mind a little breath of freedom." Dufour dropped his head and shrugged his narrow shoulders. "I fear I gave them an idea of how to change history, and they are trying to test it."

"Right, Jacques. You slipped them a historical Mickey Finn filled with speculative theories about some obscure historical figure called Franklin Roosevelt," said Currant.

Dufour leaned back in his chair and stroked his goatee. "They wanted my opinion, and I provided it. I didn't realize...."

"Go ahead, Jacques," said Wright. "Your concept?"

Dufour leaned back in his chair. His thoughts drifted back to his analysis of the 1932 American presidential election. "I saw an opening in the fabric of history in the early 1930s. America, and, in fact, the entire world, was then in the grip of a massive economic depression. The financial markets had crashed. Millions of workers were unemployed. Breadlines and squatter villages were commonplace. Events were spiraling out of control. The incumbent president in 1932 was Herbert Hoover. He was a self-made man. He was successful and intelligent and not necessarily insensitive to the needs of the citizens. But he was perceived by most people as a symbol of all the pain and misery."

"And Roosevelt?" asked Currant. "Who the hell was he?"

"Mr. Roosevelt was Governor of the state of New York. He came from money. Earlier in his career, he ran for United States vice president; before that, he was Assistant Secretary of the Navy." In short, he was part of the pampered and powerful elite that ran the country."

"A rich kid with connections, right?"

Dufour nodded. "Certainly. But in 1921, he was struck down by a horrible polio disease. He could not walk. That should have ended his political career. But instead, it seemed to mold him into a stronger, even more vital person. He never did walk again, but he and his powerful personality built a new political career, using crutches, braces, his son's strong arms, and a virtually unseen wheelchair for mobility." Dufour contemplated. "I think...but of course, this is only my guess...that he turned this personal defeat into a personal victory. And in doing so, I believe he found himself and his *raison d'être*. I also believe that somehow the people of America intuitively understood his new sense of purpose, and they would have elected him president in 1932."

"But..."

"But," said Dufour, "sadly, the election never happened. Toward the end of his campaign, there was an incident in Washington, D.C., that changed the course of history. I explained all of this to the Twins and Zak. This one event ended Roosevelt's career and put America on the path to our current destiny."

"You believe this fellow Roosevelt would have turned the country and the world around?" asked Wright.

"I think so. I've studied FDR extensively. He was very determined, and he had excellent political support from his wife, family, and advisors. I think he would have surprised both the common people and the ruling elite. The man was a consummate politician and a man of the people. He could have done it."

"What about the election?" asked Wright.

"The 1932 presidential election was canceled completely. Herbert Hoover remained the unelected President of the United States until 1936. The country was under martial law, directed by General Douglas MacArthur. For four years, the two of them ruled as a dictatorial duo. The country's economic conditions improved, and eventually, events stabilized enough to hold new elections in 1936. But the die had been cast. America had joined the growing number of major countries in the world that were run by either dictators or ruling elites. Industrial production focused on military expenditures to defend against potential enemies. The world economies were driven by the ever-present threat of war, and the people became the willing tools of repressive governments."

"And the little people?" asked Wright.

Dufour smiled and nodded. "Without power and money, the little people struggled to survive. They did what they were told willingly. They even came to enjoy the paternal qualities of a benign dictatorship. They forgot about individual freedom and replaced such thoughts with fears of the unknown. The Great Depression was over, and a New World Order began."

Currant grabbed his glass, got up, and walked to a side table. He poured another three fingers of Scotch whisky. He glanced up at the others. "Can I get you anything?"

"No, thanks, A.C., but enjoy yourself. It's now after five," said Wright, glancing at the antique mantel clock.

Currant smiled. "And what about 'Mr. Man of the People'? How did he end up after the elections were canceled in 1932?"

"Franklin Roosevelt. He became a *dilettante*. He tinkered with quite a few business schemes, even played at being an architect of sorts, but none of these efforts ever amounted to much. He lived the life of a crippled rich man, confined to a wheelchair, and drank himself to an early death in 1942."

Currant turned to Wright. "Well, you can relate to that, right, Warren?"

"Please..." said Dufour.

"Ah...don't be so serious, Dufour. Lighten up."

"A.C., you are a peach," said Wright. "Since I owe the use of my legs to you, I'll give you some latitude. While I most likely would have ended up driving my *gyromobe* for the rest of my life, you are the more likely candidate for alcoholism. Wouldn't you say?"

"Touché, my friend. I do like my scotch." Currant sipped his drink with obvious pleasure.

"We're drifting, *mes amis*," said Dufour. "The incident in 1932 that changed history. The Bonus Massacre. Twenty-two were killed in Washington, D.C., and in the riots that followed, more than three hundred fifty were killed across the nation. Martial law was declared. *Démocratique fini.* This is the historical pivot point. And this is the story I related to the Twins and Zak. I believe this is their destination."

"I remember...Mr. Weams' tenth-grade contemporary history class...it's all coming back, Jacques," said Currant, holding his right hand to his forehead as if he were channeling the answer from invisible forces. "The Bonus Marchers were war vets who camped out in D.C. in the summer of 1932. In the middle of the Great Depression. They hoped to get some money from the government. But Congress refused. President Hoover feared a riot and ordered the squatters to be removed from the city. The Army was called out to break up the camp. A bomb exploded, killing two soldiers. That started a melee. Lots of dead. Marchers, bystanders, and babies. Very nasty. J. Edgar Hoover, the head of the Bureau of Investigation, blamed the entire incident on the Communists. After that, it was all downhill. Bing, bang, boom."

"That is so, A.C. Your memory is pretty good for a seventy-seven-year-old," said Dufour.

Currant chuckled. "Like a good whisky, I only get better with age." He returned to his chair.

"Well, if we know exactly where they're going, why can't we use your *TimeTravelle* to return and get them?" asked Wright, looking over to Currant.

"No can do, Sherlock," said Currant. "One trip at a time. That's it. The youngsters have the car tonight, Warren. All we can do is sit tight. Have a drink. Relax. Those kids are smart and resilient. Of course, I have concerns about what they might do to *The History,* whether they can avoid the time cops, and whether they'll be able to return. I hope they make it back to their flight positions before the twenty-eight-day time limit." Currant stretched his neck and shrugged his shoulders.

"You're not very encouraging, A.C. That machine of yours is dangerous. Why couldn't you keep it under lock and key?"

"Sure. Blame it on me because I like to take occasional joyrides in the *TimeTravelle.*"

"What about it?"

Currant rolled his eyes. "Last week, I traveled to 1952. I took in a movie at the Mystic Theater downtown. *High Noon* with Gary Cooper. Had dinner and a few drinks with a nice-looking blonde at an old roadhouse just outside of town on the coast road. A lot of fun. Great movie. Unfortunately, when I came back, I may have forgotten to log out of the *TimeTravelle.* I was feeling the effects of my evening of entertainment. Maybe I had one too many. What's the difference? I might have opened the door, but your kids and Zak did the deed. Not me. I'm just a...."

Wright interrupted. "OK, A.C. Forget it. I guess there's nothing we can do. Do you think they know what they're doing? Can they run your time machine?"

Currant laughed. "I doubt it. Not exactly Tom Swifties, but they know enough to get into trouble. That son of yours leads with his head. Straight into trouble. Zak is smart, strong, and, I guess, super-intuitive, but he's always out for a good time. Bit of a playboy. Your best bet is Emma. She's got a real head on her pretty shoulders. I think they may stay out of trouble as long as she's in the mix."

Wright pursed his lips without responding. Finally, he shook his head and said: "They're gone..." His words trailed off as he lowered his head to his chest.

Across the table, aged physicist Currant was feeling the effects of the whisky and may have finally understood Wright's pain as he leaned against the back of his chair, took a deep breath, and exhaled loudly. "Not good," he mumbled to himself. "Not good."

The quiet room grew quieter. The antique mantel clock ticked away the time second by second. Dufour sensed the two had nothing left in them. They were spent. Fifteen rounds of circular argument had sucked the life out of the combative and frustrated friends. Right now, whatever that means, the Twins and Zak might be eating dinner nearby in a downtown Mystic Heights restaurant separated just a few hundred meters in space but a hundred years in time. Ethan, Emma, and Zak were out of reach and isolated in time.

Chapter II

Occupy the Hill

Jack Travers watched history unfold like a dirty handkerchief. He surveyed the six thousand protesters who occupied the grounds surrounding the U.S. Capitol building. Quiet but determined and restless, they nervously anticipated the Senate's decision. Travers knew that even a tiny flame of perceived injustice could ignite their indignation. It could happen today, June 17, 1932, tomorrow, or next month. The residents of Washington, D.C., and the nation's people anticipated that this mob of dissatisfied war veterans would explode into violence if the government ignored them. Travers knew the explosion was coming; someone or something was bound to light the fuse. There were just too many angry men stewing in one spot.

Not far away, on the other side of the river, thirteen thousand additional marchers were bottled up on its banks. They occupied a Hooverville, a hellhole of a tent city, in Anacostia Flats, the home of the Bonus Army. At the moment, this second group of World War veterans was temporarily unable to join their brothers-in-arms because nervous police armed with Tommy guns had raised the drawbridge across the river, blocking their way to the Capitol. But Jack Travers knew these soldiers had experienced worse hardships and had overcome far more significant obstacles in the killing fields of France. They were not rabble but organized, dedicated, and proud veterans who wanted their money now, not in 1945.

They were desperate, jobless victims of the Great Depression. The United States government had promised them a bonus, a little more than a dollar for each day of their overseas service. For most, it would amount to only a few hundred dollars; for some, maybe a thousand. But in this time of massive unemployment and national hardship, and as they viewed the world from the bottom of the economic barrel, this "bonus," as it was called by Congress, could mean the difference between life and death for them and their families. They had fought 'The War to End War'; now, a decade and a half later, they were ready for their final battle for self-respect and redemption.

Travers walked between the milling men. In their early thirties, most were just a few years older than him, but they looked older; life in America in 1932 was a sharp stick in the eye and blackjack to the back of the head. Their eyes betrayed their condition, glazed and darkened by the blackness of reality. Even Jack Travers was moved by this vision of helplessness. He let this trickle of emotion pass. Travers was not about to be sucked into the humanity of it all. He had a job to do, and misguided sympathy, even if well-intentioned, was not in his employment contract.

Travers climbed the Capitol steps. The sun lay low in the sky. Its heat, stored in the stones of the legislative fortress, created a primitive oven roasting those inside and out. Sweating senators debated. Two days earlier, the House of Representatives had passed the Bonus Bill. But without Senate approval, the bill would die. The mass of men outside remained in place, awaiting a decision. During the long day, they chanted and waved banners and signs, like the ones that read *No Pay, All Stay,* and *War Is Hell But Loafing Is Worse.* Then they would go quiet, their voices only a murmur. Then singing would spontaneously arise and again diminish to nothing. Jack Travers thought they were like mourners at their own wake, playing the parts of both the deceased and the bereaved.

The police appeared tired and nervous, holding their positions in front of each door. Some carried riot guns, some rifles, and others only holstered pistols. Time was running out. The day was ending. Travers stopped at the top of the stairs and talked to two men he assumed were veterans. They were both skinny. Their narrow faces were etched with lines, and their sunbaked skin formed tight masks of pain. One wore a working man's cap. His soiled white shirt was damp with sweat. The other was a tall man who held his beat-up blue suit coat over his arm like a shield. He had a wild, unkempt head of hair. They looked bone-tired. Their appearance resulted from their trek to Washington with weeks of riding the rails, scratching for meals, and sleeping out of doors. These were tough, proud men accustomed to hard living in strange places, but their campaign for a few dollars and some justice had drained them of their strength and patience.

"Hello, fellows. Hot one today," said Travers. He stood a couple of steps below to talk at eye level.

They looked up into the dying sun and squinted to make out the intruder, but they did not respond.

It was his suit, thought Travers. To them, he looked like a cop, or worse, a federal agent. "Jack Travers," he said. He didn't expect them to return the greeting with their names. And he didn't press them. He handed a business card to the tall one. "I'm here on special assignment on behalf of Governor Franklin Roosevelt. You've heard of him, haven't you?" Travers smiled.

The man thumbed the card and passed it to the other. Their faces remained blank. "Right. We've heard of him. Another politician. They've got lots of them in this town. Flock of 'em right behind us in the Senate building. What are you doing here? Spying on the competition? Or just gathering votes?" He snorted lightly.

"*Jack Travers, Special Assistant,*" said the other, reading the card. "You some kind of cop?"

"No, I'm not. Can I sit down?"

"Free country," said the smaller man. "Least it was this morn'."

Travers climbed the stairs and sat next to them. Slightly bent over, he held his fedora in front of him by the brim in the fingers of two hands. He scanned the thousands of men who surrounded them and then looked back at the two. Removing a pack of Luckies from his shirt pocket, he offered them up. He rarely smoked, but he found that cigarettes would often break the conversational ice and be helpful in his quest to secure information. Both men accepted his offer, and he tossed them a pack of matches with a *"Roosevelt-Garner 1932"* ad on the cover. They lit up, sucking in the smoke deeply with great pleasure. He handed them the cigarette pack. "Keep them. My throat's killing me. I've got to get off cigarettes for a while."

"Thanks." The man pocketed the pack and gave his friend a look and a nod as if to say, "Don't worry. We'll split them," or maybe that look said, "This guy's OK." Either way, Travers' gift seemed to reduce tensions.

"So what's going to happen?" asked Travers. "What happens if the senators don't pass the bill?"

The tall man stared at him, waiting for the answer to bubble up to his lips from some unknown place.

"We'll see...."

The other guy was less circumspect. "Trouble," he said, looking down at the card. "Trouble, Mr. Travers. Some kind of trouble. We didn't travel two thousand miles to lose this fight. We'll stay here 'til Thanksgiving if we need to. But we're gonna get what they promised us."

"You know, Mr. Roosevelt is very interested in your cause. He could help you," Travers looked them each in the eyes to cement this thought.

They both chuckled.

"Mister, I'm sure you mean well, but the only thing we want is our bonus. And we're not waiting for the election to see who wins. We don't care who wins. We just want our bonus," said the tall one.

Travers looked at the man. His eyes betrayed no anger, only pain. Trouble was coming, thought Travers. He knew that the life would be sucked out of these men and all their brothers after the Senate voted. And he knew the bill would never pass. He stood up and waved goodbye. They both just nodded.

While the veterans waited for the next few hours, Jack Travers interviewed many men. He was trying to gauge

their will to persevere, continue living in the miserable
conditions of the nearby temporary camps, and hold out,
waiting. Waiting for what, he wondered. This was a dead
deal; there would be no bonus. The marchers would be
faced with a decision to stay or leave. Staying was
meaningless because the political leaders who made
decisions would be heading home for vacation. Leaving
was meaningless because these men had nowhere to go
and nothing to do. Their situation was hopeless.

Mrs. Roosevelt was very concerned about their plight.
She was the reason why Travers was here. For her, the
marchers symbolized everything wrong with the United
States. They were good, strong men, ready and able to
work for a living. They had fought for this country. Now
they were fighting to survive. Travers wondered whether
Mrs. Roosevelt's husband would take on the cause as
president. He doubted it. Franklin Roosevelt was
pragmatic. Public protest such as this, directed at his
political opponent, was always valuable, but he could not
and would not encourage these men. Travers had
discovered that President Hoover suspected the whole
Bonus March event was created by the Democrats to
defeat him in the upcoming November election. This
wasn't true, but it was a good indication of the country's
mindset.

The marchers were pushing the limits of the law, and
they had everyone's attention. They brought this city to
the edge of violence. Politically, Roosevelt couldn't
publicly support the marchers, even if he believed in their
cause. The hot potato was in Hoover's hands, and
Roosevelt was quite content to let him deal with it. Travers
suspected Roosevelt was enjoying the battle of wills:
marchers versus Hoover. The lowlands adjacent to the
Anacostia River were home to the most celebrated
Hooverville in the country: a slapdash assemblage of
tents, shacks, and other temporary housing for the
veterans and, in some cases, their families.

Roosevelt could not obviously take advantage of this
situation. He would allow the current administration to

shoot itself in the foot. People around the country might sympathize with the marchers, but everyone, including President Herbert Hoover, had problems in the summer of 1932. It was difficult to gauge the intensity of public support for the veterans. Marching on Washington was a foreign concept to the average man and woman on the street. The country was stricken with a massive inferiority complex, believing that individual citizens, the "little" men and women, were somehow responsible for their helpless situation. They were ashamed of themselves, and they blamed themselves. But in fact, the economic system in America and worldwide was broken. The lost and jobless were simply victims.

His interviews over, Jack Travers was done for the day. Night had fallen. He checked his wristwatch: 9:52 p.m. He was tired. He understood the situation. He wanted to return to his room. Maybe it wasn't too late to catch a movie that night, something light, perhaps one featuring Busby Berkeley's dancers. He needed something to cut through and erase the memory of the misery that surrounded him. He walked past the marchers, who seemed to be in a trance as they stumbled along endlessly. With sadness in his heart, he tipped his hat to them. No one noticed except two men directly in his path as he crossed the street. Of course, Jack Travers had "made" these two much earlier. Clean-cut, their white shirts, ties, dark business suits, and gleaming patent leather shoes had given them away. Both men were tall: one was built like a basketball player, the other a fullback. Even though it was too hot today to wear a suit coat, they did. They didn't have a choice. Travers recognized them, and he was ready. These two were the *other* Hoover's boys, J. Edgar, as he now called himself, the 37-year-old head of the Bureau of Investigation. No stranger to bureaucracy, Jack Travers would have all the answers to their questions.

"Gentlemen." He politely and firmly tossed that single word to them like a little verbal bouquet. His broad smile exposed a perfect set of whiter-than-white teeth that combined perfectly with his pencil mustache and neatly coiffed, slick hair. He also wore a suit, tie, and vest. Quite spiffy, his dark gray pin-striped suit, unlike theirs, was perfectly fitted to his body. He looked as if he had studied John Gilbert's movies and captured his look because that is precisely what he had done.

They responded, "Bureau of Investigation." Like a coordinated dance move, the two men flashed their leather-bound credentials at Travers and just as quickly slipped them back into their jackets.

He pulled out a business card and handed it to one of the men. "Jack Travers. I work for Mr. Roosevelt."

The "basketball player" agent studied the card, searching for hidden meaning. Then he sputtered, "We were wondering about your interest in these men, Mr. Travers. We noticed you moving about in discussions with them all afternoon."

"And you thought I was a Communist?" Travers smiled at each man individually.

"We're not calling anyone names. These marchers have been known to associate with such people. Some of these veterans are really Communists. Our job is to monitor their activities and determine if any outside agitators may have infiltrated their organization."

"A noble quest. And how might I help you?"

The "fullback" agent moved closer to Travers, attempting to dominate the six-foot-tall Travers with his four-inch height advantage. "Well, for one, you could explain your interest in these men. Why have you spent most of the day working the crowd?"

Casually, Travers leaned back and struck a cavalier pose. "Just talking to my fellow Americans. Like you, we are interested in knowing their motivations and goals. It's not often that tens of thousands of men come to Washington from all corners of the country and camp out on the doorstep of the Capitol. With some luck, Mr. Roosevelt may deal with these fellows next year. They seem to have their heads on their shoulders. And they don't appear threatening to me. But then again, you're the judge of that. That's your job." He smiled again. "My job is to understand the issues and convey that understanding to Mr. Roosevelt. What do you think? Is this going to turn into something ugly?"

The basketball player grimaced. "Can't say." He glanced at his partner with a look that suggested the interview was done. The fullback nodded in confirmation. The agent turned back to face Travers. "OK, Mr. Travers, we'll be in touch if we need to talk again. Where are you staying in town?"

"I'm staying at a private residence."

At that moment, the crowd activated. Jack Travers looked back up the steps of the Capitol. Standing at the very top was a man that he recognized as Walter Waters, a veteran, former Army sergeant, and now the leader of the marchers. Waters was speaking, but his voice was too distant to be heard. Then as if a bleak cold wind of pain had blasted into the area, a groundswell of groans and shouts swept through the gathering of men. Some threw their hats to the ground in fits of anger or despair. Others simply held their heads in their hands, knowing they were beaten. Travers looked at the federal agents and said, "We'd better get out of here. They may find you, and maybe even me, an easy target for their rage. Agreed?"

He didn't have to wait long for an answer. The Bureau men saw that the crowd, first overwhelmed with grief, was now producing sounds of anger. "You're making sense, Travers. We'll see you again. That is…if you are staying in town."

"I'm staying. I'll be here until the bitter end," said Travers.

The two federal agents grabbed the brims of their hats almost in unison and gave them a tug. Then they turned tail and headed back to their offices, no doubt to report back to J. Edgar Hoover in triplicate. Travers laughed to himself. Cops, he thought, always the same, everywhere he went. Very predictable. Usually late. Incredibly officious. And almost always ineffective and unavailable when you need them. He looked around at the marchers and sized them up. These men weren't going to cause any trouble, at least not tonight. At this moment, they were nothing more than they had been when they arrived in Washington, jobless, broken, and penniless men. Only now, their cause had been summarily dismissed by the highest decision-makers in the land. The Army bonus had been officially rejected by the Senate. Strangely, the marchers had quieted, and then, even more strangely, they began to sing. Thousands of hot, tired, utterly disappointed men sang in unison "America the Beautiful." Travers was moved by their patriotism and restraint. Not long after the final words were sung, the men began to leave the steps of the Capitol. They disbursed quietly, disorganized, walking in clumps, heads down, and heading back to their makeshift city on the other side of the river.

Travers also left. It was too late for dinner, so he went directly to his apartment. He walked steadily under the gaslights and stately trees along the sidewalks leading to his home. Even at this late hour, the air remained hot and stagnant. The street was quiet, except for stray voices drifting out of the open windows of the nearby townhouses. A distant dog barked a warning, probably activated by the footfalls of his shoes. Crickets punctuated the night. Jack Travers loved these sounds of the evening.

He carefully carried his jacket over his arm so as not to allow his silvered hip flask to drop out of its inner pocket. A man of discipline, he was not an excessive drinker, but probably every other adult in D.C carried a container of "jag juice," and Jack Travers did not want to appear anything other than a man of the people. It was essential to his job that he could blend in with the locals.

His home away from home was just a few blocks southeast of the Capitol in the English basement of a private residence on a quiet street. This apartment was centrally located and suggested and facilitated by someone on Roosevelt's staff. As Mrs. Roosevelt's eyes and ears, Travers could walk everywhere and see and hear all that was important in D.C. It offered almost all the comforts of home, along with complete privacy. Travers could enter and leave unnoticed using the side door providing direct access to the small but well-fitted combination living and sleeping room, with a full bathroom and Pullman kitchen. For most of the 1920s, the room had previously been rented to a crime reporter, Randall Solomon. Preferring the small apartment's seclusion, he wrote most of his stories away from the office and often invited players from both sides of the law to share their stories and a few forbidden alcoholic drinks. He died in bed in 1930, in the arms of one of his girlfriends. The place had remained vacant until now.

Travers was a writer too. He wrote to update his employers several times a week. And the Underwood typewriter that Solomon left behind was only a few years old and in excellent condition. It rested on a small utilitarian oak desk in the niche of a window bay. During the day, it was a bright, airy room. The window offered a sparkling view of a tiny but well-landscaped courtyard. Now the only light was provided by a colorful Tiffany desk lamp. Travers hung his jacket on the back of the desk chair and closed the drapes. After sliding off his shoes, removing his tie, and loosening his shirt collar, he pulled out the flask and poured himself a well-deserved drink. It had been a very long day. He flipped on the console radio and sat down in front of the keys of the Underwood. He sipped his whisky. The best Scotch available slid down his throat like liquid lava. He embraced the moment quietly, enjoying the rush of his drink. In the background, band music drifted out, sliding Travers into a reverie. His trance was broken by a radio announcer who mentioned the news about that evening's Senate vote: *"The Patman Bonus Bill, previously passed by the House, was defeated today by a vote of 62 to 18...."* He turned it off. Enough, he thought.

While still fresh in his mind, he would dash off a brief report describing the day's activities. He created two neatly typed pages in about half an hour and proofed them carefully. Then he folded the sheets and inserted them into an envelope. Before sealing it, he removed a small blank note card and matching envelope from his desk drawer. After pondering his thoughts, he used a fountain pen to inscribe the following: *"Mrs. Roosevelt, I look forward to a time when I can meet with you again to discuss our mutual interests...in person. Respectfully yours, Jack."*

After blotting the ink dry, he sealed the small envelope. With a flourish, he addressed it with only the letter *"E."* He dropped this into the folds of his typed report and then ran his tongue lazily across the pasted surface of the envelope. Downing the remnants of his drink, he leaned back in his chair and smiled. Tomorrow morning, as always, he would personally deliver the letter to the local post office, marked "special delivery," addressed to Mrs. Franklin D. Roosevelt at her New York City, East 65th Street residence.

-Chapter III-

Attack

"You'll be safe here, Emma."

She peered into the open door of the empty, darkened boxcar. Unpleasant smells of previous occupants lingered.

Her brother tossed three valises onto the deck of the car. "Give me a hand, Zak. Let's get Miss Muffet onto her tuffet. Hurry. We don't want to be seen."

In the distance, the train's locomotive breathed slowly, alive with steam, ready.

"Why can't I just wait in the bushes? What if it takes off before you return?" asked Emma.

"Ten minutes at the most. We'll get the food and be right back. Now give Zak your foot." Zak interlocked his hands and extended them, creating a step.

She looked at Ethan. "Brother boy…" she said, shaking her head. Emma then glanced at her friend. "OK, Zak. I'm going." She lifted her leg and placed her leather oxford shoe into Zak's linked hands. She appreciated the coveralls she wore. They were well-worn and faded for authenticity but absolutely necessary for scrambling about the wooden planks of the boxcar.

"Up she goes, Zak," demanded Ethan.

Ethan guided her body while Zak effortlessly lifted her into the car. She landed with a rough thud, straightened up, and turned back to view her two facilitators, who were already out of sight.

"Be right back.…" Ethan's deep voice trailed away as he and Zak ran down the track.

She dragged the three valises into the dark recesses of the car. She was hoping to be invisible to any passersby. Her eyes grew accustomed to the darkness, and she scooted and sat with her back against the wooden siding.

Drawing up her knees, she held them against her chest. The solitary sounds of her heavy breathing filled the hot, airless, tomb-like space. Sunlight flooded through the door. The distant breathing of the train's engine continued and seemed to connect with hers. She looked about. This boxcar, old, empty, and dirty, was deadheading to Boston, except for its illegal passengers: Emma, her brother Ethan, their good friend Zak, and hoboes and rail riders unknown to them. The area on the other side of the open door was deep in shadow. A few empty wooden crates were visible in the sunlight, but nothing beyond.

She waited. Her job was to guard their property. Right. An untrained, unarmed 21-year-old woman against the world. All of this seemed like a bad idea now. Why didn't they just take a passenger train straight to Washington? Why did they have to ride the rails like three hoboes, or maybe three Bonus Marchers? Why? Because her traveling companions, idiots that they were, wanted to "feel the pain" of Americans in 1932 and become part of their world. As Ethan said, "You can't just drop down into the past and expect to be accepted. You have to earn your stripes. You have to become a citizen of 1932 America. You must be somebody with a good backstory that people will accept."

Supposedly they were three jobless, tired, threadbare young people seeking a better life someplace else: the face of the Great Depression. They had traveled miles from their home in Mystic Heights. Up to this point, everything had gone reasonably well. Two days into the trip, last night's riding of the rails ended in this small town freight yard. Using the suspect water of a nearby pond, they cleaned up and then bought some food at a small grocery store. This train stopped just outside town, was taking water for the engine, and appeared pointed in the right direction. Zak had maps of all the routes. According to him, this one was headed for Boston. She trusted him and her brother Ethan. But now, she wanted nothing more than to see them return with the food. Then they could shut the door, stay quiet, avoid trouble, and move along. She intended to take charge of their travel arrangements when they reached Boston.

No more hobo life for her. She wanted a hot bath, a hot cup of tea, and a good book, maybe *Gone with the Wind*. No, that wouldn't reach local bookstores for another four years. Well, possibly something by Virginia Woolf. She remembered a line from *The Waves*: *"On the outskirts of every agony sits some observant fellow who points."* This was how she felt now. She would point out the obvious to the guys. No more living the life of a Bonus Marcher. It was time to enjoy the trip. She reflected as she moved deep into her bath and tea fantasy. Maybe Woolf would be too serious. Some cold but lighthearted dash of Hammett, like *The Maltese Falcon,* would be excellent. She loved the movie. It was time to read the book.

Her movie musings ended abruptly, cut short by a noise on the roof. It sounded like feet shuffling. Maybe it was Ethan or Zak, and maybe not. Her senses were now cat-like; she focused on the boxcar door, hoping to see their faces. Above, the wood planks creaked and pushed down. Something heavy was up there. Disturbed dust drifted down, dancing in the slanted sunlight of the open door. She would have thought it pretty in different circumstances, like the flakes that flitted about in the water of one of those glass snow globes, but this was no holiday gathering. She was a stranger, a trespasser, in a foreign place and time. It was a dangerous place to be. Fear crept into her mind. Her skin tingled. Something or somebody was on the roof. Then a boot dangled at the top of the door, and a few seconds later, she saw another. Then the massive body of a man wearing some kind of uniform appeared.

With both hands, he hung off the head of the door, swinging back and forth like an ape. He emitted a growling sound as he dropped into the car. Immediately he spotted her. She stood frozen: speechless, frightened, and shaking. She ran to the door to escape. But he grabbed her. She was a tall woman but no match for this ape-man. His enormous hands clamped on her biceps. He pulled her close and shook her violently. His face was in her face. Oily, reddened, and puffy, it was an ugly mass of flesh. Dark eyes and bushy brows capped his pug-dog face. She wasn't going anywhere. Sickeningly, his sour breath crawled into her nose.

"Pretty little thing you are, muffin." His voice was strangely high-pitched but gravelly. "You're ridin' my train. And you ain't paid up." His black eyes locked on hers. He smiled, exposing a snarl of yellow teeth and a gray twittering tongue. Drool oozed out of the side of his mouth. The smell of stale cigarette smoke impregnated in his clothes filled the air.

In his grip, clarity hit her like a blast of icy air. She brought up her knee quickly and forcibly. It landed roughly in his manhood, and he groaned and eased his grip. She kicked him hard in the crotch, making solid contact this time. He released her and backed off. They stood facing each other like two gladiators.

Hunched over, he glared at her. Pain contorted his face. "Wildcat, eh. I like that." He smiled. "Well, you gonna pay me now, kitty. This is my train."

She looked for a way out. But it appeared hopeless. This guy would sooner beat her to a pulp than let her go. She had never faced such a person. Nothing in her mind could help her except for memories of nasty movie scenes that had once fascinated her, but this was no movie. This was reality unleashed. She could only mumble, "Please...."

Leisurely, he removed his belt and dropped it. The attached gun and nightstick banged on the floor. The excitement in him now went beyond the physical challenge. As his eyes slowly surveyed Emma's body, his grinning mouth salivated in anticipation. She knew nothing of this. It was animalistic and prehistoric. Her knees knocked violently. She peed.

The attacker saw what happened, laughed, coughed up phlegm, and spat at her feet.

"Ethan!" she cried.

"Not my name. You can call me boss. Now get down on all fours."

She trembled and backed up. The wall stopped her. Slowly, the monster moved in on her. Instinctively, she closed her eyes and shouted out, "Ethan!" She felt his hands tighten on her waist, but she couldn't look. He spun her around. Her head hit the wall. She caught herself in a fall and stopped it with both hands leaning against the wall.

"That's it, girl. You got it." He slapped her backside hard. The pain shot through her shocked body like an electric charge. She felt his fingers reaching in, grabbing the top of her jeans from behind.

Now in a panic, bent over, she sucked in the hot, stale boxcar air in deep, painful breaths. A part of her was a witness, silently begging for help. Nausea gripped her. She pleaded quietly, "No, don't. Please, don't."

He snorted as she squirmed and whimpered. He pushed against her body, and his hot, wet breath coated the back of her neck. She screamed. Then she heard a loud crack, hardwood meeting skull bone, then another crack, then the moan of the ape-man and the sound of him falling to the floor.

She opened her eyes and saw the beast on the floor, spread-eagled, lifeless. The man who felled him stood over him still holding the nightstick, watching for any movement, ready to deliver another blow. She was shaking and filled with rage.

The diminutive but well-built man smiled broadly beneath a bulky black mustache. "Take it easy. I mean no harm. Do not be frightened." His voice was deep, melodic, and soothing.

Now she could hear her body's response to her fear: rapid breathing and her heart pulsing. She felt sick to her stomach.

"Relax," he said. "Take a breath. The bull will not be waking for a while. But he will get up. And we do not want to be here when he does. Come on. Follow me." He went to the door, pulled on it, and slid it almost closed.

Uncertain about his intentions, she didn't move. "What do you want?" she asked.

He looked over his shoulder at her. "I want out of here. Now."

Seconds passed as she looked down at the railroad cop and then back up at the man. His face bore impatience. "OK. I'm coming," she said.

Quickly, she moved to his side, and he guided her. "Back to the door. Give me your hands. Both of them. I will set you down." She followed his directions. His hands were small, but his grip was firm. "Step down and let your foot catch the ledge below. Feel for it with your toe." She faced him with her back out of the boxcar. She stepped out with one foot, searching for support, and found it. "Now the other," he said. He held her in place as her other foot found the ledge. "Now, on 'three,' jump away, and I'll let you down gently." She nodded. "One, two...three." She fell freely for an instant before his hands became handholds. He slowly held her out with incredible strength and gently lowered her down to the stone roadbed below. When her feet touched the ground, he released her, and she stumbled back away from the train. She heard three short blasts of a whistle, then the sound of the train engine coming to life. A staccato ring of metal-on-metal sounds cascaded from the front of the freight train. The boxcar jerked forward. The man tossed the three valises onto the ground and then hung out of the car with one hand grasping the doorjamb. With the other, he pulled the door closed. He motioned for her to get out of the way. Then he leaped gracefully like a lion onto the ground, rolled over twice, and stood erect in one motion.

"When the cinder dick wakes up, he will be halfway to Portland."

"Portland?" said Emma. "We just came from that direction. What about Boston?"

He smiled. "Big ugly guy did you a favor. This train not going to Boston."

Emma shrugged her shoulders. Zak had been so sure about this train. Men, she thought, always know best. If it was up to them, everyone would be riding in circles. The man grabbed her hand roughly and brought her mind back to focus.

"You carry one. I get others." He bent over and picked up the bags. Slowly, she followed his orders and grabbed the other.

"Now. We move." He pushed her forward, and they both ran into the scrub growth.

Vegetation attacked her as they stumbled onward. Bushes and branches cut and beat her as he guided her through the underbrush. After about five minutes of tortured movement, she yelled, "Stop!" They rested. Breathing heavily, they set down the bags. They both hung at the waist as she struggled to speak. "My brother and our friend. Coming back. Went to get food. Won't know where I went. We must go back."

"Forget them. You don't want to go back. Don't worry. Someone will track them down." As they rested, the man looked into the face of the young woman he had saved. "Why are you here?" He grasped her hand gently and examined her palm. "You have hands like princess. You should not be on the road." He released it and looked into her eyes.

Emma smiled. His eyes were warm and comforting. "I wish I was a princess. I'm Emma. But I'm only an unemployed social worker. We all just graduated from college, but there are no jobs. So we're going to Washington. We're going to join the war vets. To help them. They need it."

"I am Branko," he said, scrunching his face as if thinking. "I read about them in the newspapers. Many ride rails heading for Washington. Good men. Lost souls. Like me. Maybe I join you. I was heading nowhere, but...." He began moving again, walking now. "Come."

"Wait..." she said.

He looked back.

"I want to thank you. You saved me. I don't...."

He smiled. "You are princess. I am your frog. I am not a prince, so do not kiss me. I am only a man who wishes no harm to come to you."

She leaned in and gave him a soft kiss on the cheek. "Thank you, my prince."

Branko blushed. He turned. "We go now. Almost there."

"Almost where?" she asked as she walked several feet behind him.

Over his shoulder, he looked back and replied, "The Jungle."

-Chapter IV-

The Jungle

Ethan Callan-Wright pulled out his gold-plated Hamilton pocket watch and popped open the cover. He studied the watch face as if it might talk. "This is a railroad watch, Zak. It has to be right. We've only been gone about twelve minutes. What the heck could have happened in twelve minutes?"

Zak looked into Ethan's face. Of course, he couldn't talk to him because Zak was afflicted with aphasia, but he viewed himself as blessed, not afflicted. He was the biological product of the short-lived, secret, and experimental *Employ America* cloning program, which gave him movie-star looks, incredible physical strength, and extra-sensory perception, but left him without usable vocal chords. In his own time, he wore an electronic device called the *Voicenator* that allowed him to speak normally. Since it could be programmed to match any voice, he spent years experimenting with it until he adopted the voice of a 1990's movie actor. The *Voicenator* was a fantastic technological breakthrough, but it couldn't be used in the year 1932, a year in which the people of the time marveled at the recent inventions of spray-can whipped cream and the Zippo cigarette lighter. Therefore, it remained in his desk drawer back in the future. Nevertheless, Zak communicated quite well with his friends, but only with sign language. He signed: *"The train is gone, and Emma is gone. We blew it."*

Ethan lost his concentration. "You know, sometimes I wish you brought your talking necklace. I get tired of watching your words." One look at his friend and he knew he regretted his words. "Sorry. I'm just frustrated. Let's move into the bushes. We're sitting ducks out here."

They grabbed their sacks of food and made their way

down the railroad embankment, then into the dense undergrowth at the edge of the forest. Side by side, they sat on a fallen log that served as a makeshift bench. No conversation now, Ethan's mind searched for an answer. His sister was in a boxcar on a train going someplace unknown to her or them. She had been right, as usual. They should have let her hide in the bushes. But he had wanted to save time. Getting on and off trains was still a major project for them. He had thought that if she was on the train, she could help them take in the food bags quickly and minimize their exposure. But that was immaterial now. The train was gone, and so was Emma. Saving time for time travelers was critical because their available time was limited. Already, they were behind schedule. Every second had to be used productively. This flight to the year 1932 would last 28 days at most. That much they understood. But, since they really knew very little about the intricate mechanics of Dr. Currant's time machine, even that was a gamble. Ethan repeated his misgivings audibly. "Just enough to be dangerous..."

Zak looked at him quizzically.

"Sorry, I was just thinking how little we know about the time-travel business. And we know even less about this 1932 world. I thought hopping trains would be fun and easy." He shook his head. "It's really neither. Zak, we're screwed. Emma is gone. And we have no way of finding her. We don't even know where that train was heading."

Zak signed: "*South...maybe.*"

"Yeah. South where? Florida, Arkansas, Texas? South, my ass. There's nothing we can do." Ethan stood up. He bent over, picked up a big rock and threw it hard against the trunk of nearby oak tree. The sound of the impact was like a rifle shot that broke the dead quiet in the woods. Birds scattered. Little animals rustled in the undergrowth. The tree absorbed his frustration and anger. Then the forest settled, quiet again. The young adventurers stared at the rock, which had bounced back and landed at their feet. They remained lost in their thoughts, two guys in the middle of nowhere, without answers. Then, Ethan heard a twig snap. It sounded loud, near. In an instant, he knew that something or somebody was close.

The burlap bag came down over Ethan's head faster than he could react. He reached up to remove it, but just as quickly somebody grabbed his arms. Two powerful sets of hands pulled his hands behind him. He struggled. Ethan was big and powerful, a force. He fought them, but very quickly they tied his hands at the wrists. He tried to stand, but others in front of him held him down. These attackers were strong men.

"Stay put, young fellow, and nothing will happen to you," the voice was commanding, but not threatening. "Sit quietly. Like your buddy."

He guessed there were five or six men. They could have weapons. He didn't struggle anymore. He just waited. He tested the ropes on his wrists. They held fast. He assumed that his friend had also been captured. Zak might be able to break his bonds, because even though Zak looked like just a pretty boy, he was one incredibly strong person. This edge would be unexpected by their captors. That gave him some hope. The smell of the wet burlap bag was repulsive. He fought the urge to leap up and try to run. "What do you want?" he asked, his words muffled by the bag.

"I've got a better question. What the hell do you want? This is our territory. And you're not invited."

Somebody else spoke in a quiet voice. "They got food here, Jake. Two bags full."

"You guys on a camping trip? Or maybe you're railroad dicks."

"Let's take the bags and go," said a third male voice.

Ethan heard the sound of their food bags being lifted. "Wait," he said, "we're just lost. We don't work for the railroad. We don't work for anyone. We were hopping a freight with my sister and the train got away from us. She's gone now, and we need help."

No response.

"You can keep the food. We just need help. We need to know where that train was going. We have to find Emma."

Seconds passed in silence.

"Emma...eh?" said a quiet voice that sounded more human. "You're comin' with us. Git up now."

The "jungle" was a clearing in the woods. Only someone flying overhead in an airplane would have any idea it existed. Wearing the smelly burlap bags on their heads with their hands tied behind their backs, Ethan and Zak stumbled through the woods, guided only by rough directional pushes from the men. Finally, the blindfolded passage, along with the tripping, bumping, and falling down, ended. Ethan sensed they were now out of the woods. He heard many voices that grew louder as they walked.

"You can stop now, boys," said the leader.

Ethan stopped walking. All the voices quieted. Then his hood was ripped from his head. Momentarily blinded by sunlight, he blinked involuntarily. Someone cut the ropes that bound him. The release of pain and discomfort and the bright light disoriented him. Slowly, he regained his composure and his vision. He saw Zak nearby. He scanned the area. He also saw many men, sitting on boxes, stumps, and pails around a campfire. They were a sorry-looking lot. They stared at the newcomers with empty eyes. Old and young, ragged, unshaven, and bedraggled, they were obviously "forgotten men", hoboes, derelicts, bums. They had many names, but no homes, these men of the "jungle."

"Here ya go, fellows. These two punks brought some fixin's for our mulligan." As he spoke, one of the men dumped the contents of the food bags onto the ground near the large pots stewing on the open fire. A rumble of appreciation arose. Men leaped off their seats and scrambled for the tins, boxes, and bags of food.

"Hold on! We ain't no jungle buzzards."

Ethan recognized the voice as the leader of his captors. He turned to see the tall, gray-haired, hawk-faced man who issued commands. The man nodded. "Don't worry. We won't take all your food. Will we, fellows? Just enough to give some life to mulligan and feed three more mouths."

Ethan looked at Zak, who signed back: *"Three?"*

A hand grabbed Ethan roughly by the shoulder and spun him around. Ethan looked down on his attacker. This guy was a full head shorter than Ethan, probably five-foot-five at best. He filled out his tight-knit khaki sweater, all muscle, but no match for Ethan.

"What's your problem?" shouted Ethan.

"You are problem," said the man. "You left your sister. Alone in the boxcar. That is not smart."

"How do you know? What about Emma?"

"Oh. Now you care."

"Yes. She's on a train by herself. We don't know where it's going. And you're right. It was stupid."

"Tell 'em, Branko," said one of the men tending the stew.

The man called Branko looked Ethan directly in the eyes. "You take better care of your sister. Or you answer to Branko."

Ethan stumbled with his words. "I do. I mean, I did. Anyway, who are you to..."

He was interrupted by a voice coming from inside an old army-surplus tent tucked into the leafy edge of the clearing.

"Ethan."

Ethan was shaken by the sound of Emma's voice, and both he and Zak were startled when she popped out of the tent.

"You better thank this man. He saved my life." She walked rapidly to them, tall, straight, rock-solid, and unsmiling, until she stopped directly in front of her brother. Ethan was wide-eyed and stunned. Zak grinned. "You, my dear brother, are an idiot. But I forgive you." She reached up and hugged him. Ethan grabbed her and lifted her off the ground then set her down gently. She turned to her friend and said: "And you, Mr. Zak, are just as responsible. If it wasn't for this man, I would be..." Her smile disappeared and her voice trailed off.

Zak needed no invitation. He reached out and hugged her. Quickly, he signed: "*Hijole! You OK?*"

Quietly, she responded, "*I am.*" She winked at him.

With that, Ethan knew that, at least for now, all was right in their little world.

That night, after they had eaten a bowl of some pretty good stew, and after Emma had given them a vivid description of the attack in the boxcar, she went to sleep in the tent. The shelter was courtesy of the jungle residents and recognition of the fact that she was the only woman in the camp. After her very nasty day, she fell asleep quickly. Ethan listened to her deep breathing as he and Zak lay on bedrolls nearby. Zak wrote his log by firelight while Ethan pondered the future in the land of the past. The other men were scattered about the clearing, threes and fours nestled in the grass like fugitive animals hiding from the world. The clear, black night sky was empty but for a sea of stars and the orange sparks flying upward from the crackling bonfire. Cigarette smoke drifted in the air. Ethan was reminded of their previous flight back in time four years ago. 1963 was also filled with clouds of cigarette smoke. Even though he knew such smoke was poison, he liked the smell of burning tobacco. For him, it was ceremonial incense from the past, in some ways it was strange yet comforting, but it also reminded him to be cautious and calculating in this new world. He, Emma, and Zak were the most foreign of all foreigners, time travelers. Uncertainty, surprise, and danger would always be their shadows.

Some of the men talked in muffled conversations, not yet ready for or capable of sleep. In the distance, one of the hoboes quietly played his harmonica. The day was ending for these forgotten men of the Great Depression. Some, the World War veterans in the group, would break camp tomorrow and head for the nation's capital just like the Twins and Zak. Others would stay on, living in miserable conditions, hoping for a better tomorrow. Ethan lay there contemplating the negative possibilities of Emma's encounter today. He blamed himself and resolved to be more responsible. He wondered about the man Branko. After delivering his tongue-lashing and producing Emma in startling fashion, Branko had announced to Zak and Ethan that he would be traveling with them to Washington. He didn't trust them to get Emma there safely. Ethan was in no position to argue. He had failed where Branko had succeeded. Branko apparently knew what he was doing and where he was going. Ethan fell asleep agreeing with the mysterious Branko. He knew had acted like an idiot risking her life, and he realized that Emma had a new protector.

LOG of Zak Newman

July 15, 1932 (local time): 21:00 (Day 3 of time travel)

First item: my apologies to Dr. Currant. By now, he is no doubt very upset. I'll bet he never figured we could activate the TimeTravelle by ourselves. It wasn't easy, and we were in for a surprise when we arrived in 1932. We took the same positions on the TimeTravelle as we had for the 1963 flight. And the machine delivered us to the cliff overlooking Smuggler's Cove. But, unlike our last "back door" trip, when we popped into the past this time, there was no war memorial and no chess board — only windblown grass and rocks. The place was desolate. Immediately, Ethan recognized the problem, and cautioned us not move an inch. He made us mark the outline of our feet. Then, we filled out the footprints with patterns of stones. In addition, we rolled one large rock to mark the center of the arrival point. And we carefully concealed the entire area with fallen branches. Once we marked our entry points, we moved down the hill and started our adventure. Our goal was to change history — mucho grande.

Dr. Currant can guess our flight plan because he and Professor Dufour know our intentions. Of course, I'm sure he thinks this whole thing is a total waste of time and dangerous. Admittedly our efforts to save JFK fell short four years ago, but we still believe we did have a positive impact on history. Let's hope we are at least as successful on this flight. If we can stop the Bonus March massacre from happening, maybe there will be no nationwide martial law; no suspension of the presidential elections; and no quasi-dictators in the White House. With some luck, Dufour's boy — Franklin Delano Roosevelt — will be elected, and the world will be a better place.

Nobody really knows what he will do if elected, but we'll see. Maybe he's just another rich-guy politician. But he has to be better than the fascist fumblers who stole the election. They screwed up history and our lives big time. After 1932, everyone knew that push comes to shove, the big bad rich guys would jump in and take control whenever they got nervous about their future. They did it again in 1963, giving our buddy JFK a very painful headache. Ethan loves that old Rolling Stones' song "Under My Thumb." He thinks it fits the mindset of "the controllers" who run the planet in 2032. Emma doesn't like the sexist lyrics, no matter what. And me, I like the old punk band Social Distortion's version. I think their music captures the essence of the historical battle for world domination.

Even considering all that we have been through today, this night is strangely peaceful. I'm comforted by a deep layer of time that separates me from the world of 2032. I feel like Thoreau residing at the edge of his placid pond away from civilization and its painful tensions. There is no tension here. These men, rejected by the economic machine, have become strangers in their own land. They survive on the tattered edges of the American Dream, moving from place to place like a bewildered herd. Some gathered here are truly forgotten men; others are simply hoboes. The "'bos" were living this life before October 1929 and will probably continue on this way to the end. Like nomads, they live day to day, wandering and piecing together a fragmented existence. The former desk jockeys, truck drivers, and farmers who have joined the homeless and hopeless in this part of the "Jungle" may still have something left of their dreams. Who knows? And then there are the Bonus Marchers. We've got five or six in camp.

I listened to their discussions as they talked around the campfire tonight. Some are as new to this process of train-hopping as Ethan, Emma, and I. But, even though they are rookies in this game, they are all former military men. Older guys who fought in the World War. Tough guys. Not long ago, they were responsible citizens earning a living and paying their taxes. They stand out from the ever-listless, homeless, and abandoned. These men are disciplined. They have a history and a goal. They have "God on their side." They are going to Washington, D.C., to make their elected representatives release the money that was promised to them.

We will join them in their travels tomorrow. We're all going to Washington. Including, it appears, Branko, the man who saved Emma. The word around camp is that he is a former circus acrobat of some fame. But he, too, is out of work. Listening to his conversations tonight, he seems to have adopted the Bonus Marchers' cause as his own. He also seems to have taken on Emma as his responsibility. I'm afraid Ethan and I do not quite measure up to his standards as protectors. And maybe he is right. It was foolish for us to leave her alone. The three of us must stay together because we always travel alone, even when surrounded by others of this time.

End 07-15-32

Chapter V

Dollars to Doughboys

After several days living in boxcars, the four travelers reached their destination. Along with five war veterans who had arrived on the same train, they hitched a ride in the back of a produce truck and were dropped off at the Anacostia River, a garbage-filled, stagnant inlet of the Potomac. Marching in line with the former soldiers, they crossed the river on a long, narrow drawbridge connecting the patch of ground occupied by the marchers to the central section of Washington, D.C. As they marched, the veterans sang one of their now-familiar songs. This one was aimed at Wall Street: "Mellon pulled the whistle, Hoover rang the bell, Wall Street gave the signal. And the country went to hell!"

Zak and Ethan chuckled. "Who's this guy Mellon?" asked Ethan.

Zak signed back, "*Secretary of the Treasury.*"

"Right. Head man. 'Mr. Big Business,'" said Ethan, recalling foggy bits of a long-lost college history class. "But no friend of the common man."

A short walk brought them to their destination. Ethan was stunned by his first vision of the cardboard and canvas construction at the Bonus Marchers' camp. Contained by the river on one side and a low embankment on the other, this narrow slot of humanity looked like picnic grounds in a junkyard. But it was home to more than ten thousand men, women, and children. Combined with the other D.C. marcher locations, the population of this new virtual city matched that of real 1932 cities like Vancouver, Washington, and Boise, Idaho. It was a giant Hooverville shantytown unlike any other in the country. The hot, swampy site on the Anacostia River, just across from the capital city of the United States of America, was occupied by veterans of the World War fought in Europe. They were the American Expeditionary Force when fighting and dying for America. They turned the tide of the war by defeating Germany and changing the course of history. They were a proud, organized, dedicated fighting machine. But that was yesterday, and yesterday's gone, thought Ethan. Today, they are nothing more than a crowd of discarded, almost burned-out men huddled together, grasping at straws. They came here for their bonus money. As in 1917 and 1918, they had a cause to rally them. But the righteousness of this cause was not enough to change the conditions of their lives. Two months ago, they were jobless, hungry men living in places like Milwaukee, Seattle, Atlanta, and New York City. Now they were unemployed, hungry men living on mosquito-infested swampland at the doorstep of the nation's capital.

Ethan, Emma, Zak, and Branko walked under a makeshift wooden archway bearing a hand-painted overhead sign: *B.E.F. White House.* Hundreds of shanties, tents, and tarpaper shacks were strewn about. These temporary shelters lined both sides of randomly placed muddy roads. Dogs and little tykes ran about; smoke drifted up from cooking fires; half-dressed men washed their bodies with water from tin buckets; and others milled about, stumbling over the uneven, muddy surface of the "flats," the name given to this useless piece of land by the locals.

"B.E.F.?" questioned Emma.

"Bonus Expeditionary Force, Emma," answered Branko. "Maybe we meet some fellow travelers here. Here everyone is one of us."

"Rail riders?" asked Emma.

Branko thought, then nodded. "And without job. And hungry."

Zak ran ahead of the group and signed back at them, "*When do we eat?*"

Branko appeared befuddled. While they traveled, he had attempted to communicate with Zak on the most rudimentary of topics without success. Zak's inability to speak and Branko's lack of knowledge of sign language put a quick end to all discussion.

"Our friend is hungry, Branko. And I am, too," said Ethan. "Let's find someplace to grab a bite."

Before anyone could contemplate their next move, they were approached by three men. Ethan was impressed. These guys looked undernourished and scrawny but almost as tall as him, a rarity for 1932. Immediately, they directed the five war veterans to a nearby welcoming tent, but they held up the Twins, Zak, and Branko. They quickly surmised that the young woman and the three men who accompanied her were not war vets. Eyeing the four travelers carefully, they inquired as to their business. Ethan figured they were on the lookout for troublemakers. He acted as spokesman for the group and informed them that they supported the cause of the Bonus Marchers and wished to be allowed to help in any way possible. The men were cautious. The conversation was short. They were asked to follow one of the camp cops.

The four walked rapidly through the maze of tents and huts. The military policeman led the way, and the others followed behind. The little safari proceeded quickly to an open area near the river, possibly an assembly place. The MP yelled out to stop. Ethan looked back. His sister had fallen behind and was shaking the mud off her shoes. She gave Ethan a look of disgust but then regrouped and continued the trek.

Ethan's view of the river, and the city of Washington, D.C., on the other side, was obscured by the low morning haze rising from the hot, marshy grounds. Except for the mud, the ramshackle shelters, and the scruffy former soldiers, the scene was somewhat picturesque. Beyond the edge of the field and the scattered trees that lined the river, the white stone buildings of the nation's capital, like massive sentinels, poked through the translucent haze. The lead man stopped at the opening of a large tent. Ethan heard loud, intense voices coming from inside.

"We didn't come three thousand miles to give up!"

"We're not giving up, but we've done all we can. Congress is gone, and they're about to kick us out. We've overstayed our welcome, Joe. Now go pass out these flyers. We have to get these men back to their homes."

"What homes?"

"Just do it."

"Yes, sir." A heavy, red-faced man shot out of the tent carrying a handful of flyers. He hurriedly handed flyers to the MP and Branko as he passed. "General Butler will have something to say about this...." He muttered this statement under his breath, talking to himself.

Ethan caught a quick glance at the flyer copy headlined *Bulletin*. The MP poked his head into the tent, nodded to the travelers, and directed them inside. A thin, gaunt, handsome man dressed in khaki jodhpurs and a battle-dress shirt stood behind a makeshift desk. He had a cigarette pack tucked into his right shirt pocket and a couple of military medals dangling from his left pocket. His polished calf-high cavalry boots were spattered with mud. Except for his rigid bearing, he had that same war-stained, world-weary look that Ethan saw in almost every man in the camp. It was a look of experience, determination, and will.

"What do we have here?"

"Newcomers, sir. Civilians," said the MP.

Walter W. Waters looked over his new guests. "Who's the leader here?" His voice was raspy.

The quartet looked at each other, seemingly stumped by the question. The pause turned into embarrassing emptiness. Then Ethan and Emma started speaking at the exact moment. Then they stopped.

Waters smiled. "Good thing you're not in the Army. Indecision and unclear command. A certain path to defeat."

Ethan grabbed the conversational reins. "Right. I'm Ethan. My sister Emma. This is Zak. And this is Branko. We arrived today on a freight train with some of your new recruits. We're here because we want to honor your cause and help."

"I'm Commander Waters. I run the B.E.F. You're a little late. Our work is done here. We'll be heading home as soon as possible."

"We want to help. We'll do anything. And we could use a place to stay. We'll earn our keep."

"This encampment is for veterans and their families. That's it."

Emma stepped forward. "Commander. We've traveled hundreds of miles, and we're really determined to be part of your cause. I've been educated as a social worker. We're not soldiers. But we're unemployed. We're young and strong. And we are resourceful. There must be something we can do to ease the burdens of these men and their families."

Waters studied each of the travelers in sequence. "You're not Communists, are you?"

Ethan laughed. "Nope. Just good old-fashioned Americans." He glanced at his fellow travelers. His eyes stopped at Branko. "Except maybe for Branko. He's Serbian. But he saved my sister's life when she was attacked by a railroad cop."

"College kids?"

Ethan nodded. "Used to be. But now we're just part of the great wandering herd."

Waters' eyes drifted to Branko. "What about you? You look a little long in the tooth for 'boula boula.'"

"I do not...." Branko stammered.

"What's your work? What's your job?"

Branko thought for a moment and then stiffened. "I was in circus in my homeland. Trapeze. Tightrope. Tumbling. But that life is gone. I am here also to help." Branko's heavy accent made him difficult to understand but enhanced his sincerity.

Waters scanned the three men. Seconds passed. "I may have some work for you." He wore a wry smirk. Then he spoke quickly and quietly. "You know we have over ten thousand people here. We have diarrhea, dysentery, and influenza. This is no picnic. But if you're game, OK. The

MP will show you to the Sweeny family's tent. They need help. They've got three young ones. You can stay the night, but then you will have to find other accommodations. If you prove to be of any use, you can come back and help during the day. But when I tell you to leave for good...you will leave. Understood?"

"Right," said Ethan.

His voice rose. "Latrine duty for the men," he ordered. "The young lady can assist Mrs. Sweeny in the Indiana section." In seconds, they were ushered out by the MP.

Outside the tent, Zak signed to Emma: "*Latrine duty?*"

"Welcome to Camp Marks," she said, laughing. And one by one, like a small platoon, they followed the MP through the camp.

-Chapter VI-

The Forgotten Family

The Sweeny "residence" was a disjointed contraption of old canvas, scrap wood, and cardboard, just one small, leaky lifeboat in the middle of hundreds of similar jumbles of junk floating uncomfortably on the muddy flats of the Anacostia. The sleeping area, a patched and tattered army-issue tent, had a skimpy, mud-caked tarp as flooring. Cotton sack mattresses stuffed with hay, active with bedbugs, and set directly on the soggy tarp, served as bedding. With its roof of rotted board timbers covered with dirty old carpets and mats, the living and kitchen area was even less protective. The Sweeny home had all the qualities of a pigsty. The exterior walls were clad with an ersatz appliqué of scavenged paper products, and rainwater channeled haphazardly onto the ground below created perpetual mud and muck. The windows, hacked-out openings in the cardboard, provided portals to the outside misery. But, except for the heat and darkness, there was little difference between the inside and outside. Emma was disheartened by the overall living conditions of the camp. There was just one shower for all Camp Marks, no hot water, and only very crude toilets. Her male counterparts were gone; Ethan, Zak, and Branko had been directed to muck out the latrines. For once, she was pretty content with her feminine status.

Now, the family Sweeny was her concern. While she and Emma did chores, Mrs. Sweeny related the story of the family's journey to Washington. Hitchhiking, rail-riding, and walking, they managed to travel six hundred miles from Gary, Indiana, to Washington, D.C. John Sweeny formerly worked at a steel plant. Until 1930, he had sound employment as a night shift supervisor in the sheet mill. His wife Molly had cared for the children and

run the household in a tiny, rented frame bungalow on the east side of Gary. The steel mill was shut down now, and John was out of work, as he had been for nearly two years. Emma, Ethan, and Zak knew something else about the family Sweeny. They would soon be part of the Bonus Massacre, participants in the coming carnage.

Emma struggled with washing clothes by hand in a large galvanized metal tub. It was backbreaking work. She stirred the mixture of soap, lye, and water, worked the clothes over the wood-framed galvanized washboard, and wrung them out; then she got more water for rinsing from the single available tap, stirred and wrung again, and finally, she strung up the clothes on the sagging hemp rope that stretched from the Sweenys' hovel to the adjacent shack. She rested often and gazed out the gaping cardboard opening at the front.

Children ran and played like kids everywhere, oblivious to the harsh environment. Former soldiers walked about the camp, usually in pairs or threes. She noticed that segregation between the races was non-existent in Camp Marks. Colored men, as they were called, shared duties and rations with white men side by side. This was different from the scenes she had witnessed in the South 31 years later in 1963. Poverty and war were the great equalizers, she thought. The Sweenys' dog, a frisky young German shepherd with three good legs and a stump for the fourth, would often limp into their shelter, investigate her activity, and then hop out to play with the Sweeny children. The kids overlooked his handicap as they repeatedly made him run and retrieve a stick. The dog never gave up. Mr. Sweeny called him Bosch, a nickname for German soldiers in the war, because he said they never gave up either. She caught glimpses of Molly and her three children. The five-year-old, Michael, played in the mud with his three-year-old sister, Brenda. They were constructing some kind of miniature town out of sticks and stones. Molly Sweeny wore the 3-month-old baby of the family, Colleen, across her chest like permanent infant armor. She held her in place with her left arm and completed her chores using her right arm. There was no place in their shelter to safely leave the baby alone, so the little girl was always carried. After Emma hung the last pair of pants on the line, she dragged out a wooden orange crate and sat down on it. She was exhausted; she gazed at the kids at play, only half-listening to their running commentary about their imaginary Irish village. A shadow crossed her line of vision, sliding her back into the moment.

"Thank you for the canned milk for the children. They haven't had much in the way of treats since we arrived here. Your milk and crackers were just what they needed," said Molly Sweeny.

Emma just nodded.

"I'd guess you had enough, Emma."

Emma gazed up at the woman. "I don't know how you do it, Molly. I simply do not know," she talked slowly, her voice tentative. "Why don't you just pack up and leave? This is impossible."

Molly swept back her lengthy, black, frizzled hair with her free hand. Her baby napped calmly on her chest, unaware of the squalor and pain surrounding her. With a sigh, she sat on the beat-up front seat of an old automobile that served as a lounge chair. "I've had that conversation with John. Just about every day of our stay in this place. But he is a man of conviction. He will stay the course."

"But Congress has rejected the Bonus Bill and left town. Nothing good will happen. It would be better to leave now before they kick you out. I've heard they're offering some kind of transportation home."

"Heard that myself. Believe me, I am tired. But we have no home to go back to. We have nothing. Nothing but this junk pile behind you. We used to have things. We thought we had a future. But we were wrong."

"But..."

"Emma, I am thankful for your help and the food you brought us, but I'm a mother and a wife. My husband wants to stay. We will stay."

"He's the boss, right?" asked Emma.

"He is my man, Emma. What about you? What's a pretty young woman like you doing here? Don't you have a fellow back home?"

Emma hesitated. "No...I don't."

"They must be lining up for your hand, dear. What's the problem?"

"Well, I just think there is more to life than getting married and having children." After saying this, Emma wanted to take it back. She could see Molly was offended.

"Oh. You're one of them," said Molly.

"Them?"

"You know...a modern woman."

Emma reflected. "I guess you would say I am very modern." She smiled. "But I meant no disrespect, Molly. I just haven't found the right person. It's difficult, you know."

"That's OK. I understand. A lot of young folks are thinking the same thing. Why get married and have a family when you can't even support them properly?" Looking out from the front of her cardboard home, she watched her two youngsters playing with trash. Her eyes glistened with pain. Then she appeared to regroup mentally. "Of course, John is the head of the family. But since he lost his job, he hasn't been well. Sometimes he is a difficult man. His mother said that the war changed him. John fought in the trenches in France. I didn't know him then, but he's always been somewhat melancholy and anxious. Many war vets are like that. They don't talk about what happened over there. I know John won't. But they remember. He doesn't sleep well. Very bad dreams. And sometimes he forgets where he is. But I love the man. And I will stand by him to the end." She looked around. "Even in this godforsaken place...." Her voice and face dimmed.

Emma stood up and took the baby from the woman. She looked into its tiny, round, pink, innocent face. "She is the sweetest little baby. Don't keep her on this island of hell, Molly. This place is dangerous for her and everyone. Leave while you can. I can give you some money to help you. Please consider leaving now before it is too late. You must have somebody you can stay with for a time. Somebody, someplace."

Molly chuckled. "I appreciate your concern, but we'll get on. And there is nobody who wants us. That's why we are here. That's why all these people are here. These are forgotten men, and we are a forgotten family."

"No matter what, I will come and help you. Every day if I can."

"Thank you, dear. Thank you. God bless you." Molly turned away and gazed across the shacks and shanties that littered the Anacostia flats, and then she focused on the brilliant white stone obelisk in the distance. The Washington Monument reflected the sinking sun's rays into her glistening eyes. "Land of the free. Home of the brave," she muttered. "What happened to the dream, Emma? What happened?"

Emma, Ethan, Zak, and Branko stayed with the Sweeny family that night. Molly made dinner with the food that Emma had purchased outside the camp. The meal was hot and simple and cooked on a grate over an open fire. All through dinner, Branko acted like a grandparent to the Sweeny children. They were entertained by his stories of life in the circus. Emma listened to him as he captured the little ones' hearts with his wild tales of lions, tigers, and elephants. He told about the freaks, the sideshows, and the games of chance. "We told the suckers: 'Knock down the bottles and win a cigar.' They were always close...but no cigar. They paid and played again and again and lost over and over." He said it sadly as if he was imparting his vision of his life and the world.

Emma liked Branko; he was different in how he talked and acted, but she could tell he had a good heart. After dinner, little Michael was particularly amazed at Branko's acrobatic tricks, which involved having the young boy standing on the Serbian's shoulders as he balanced on one foot. Over the begging complaints of the children, Mrs. Sweeny tucked them into bed, and soon they were asleep. Both Molly and John Sweeny thanked the foursome for their help, particularly Branko, for providing some overdue amusement and diversion for their children.

Not long afterward, Branko unveiled a bottle of bootlegged whisky that he had tucked away in his knapsack. The adults went out front and sat on boxes around a small campfire. They were joined by the dog, Bosch, who circled once and then sat at his master's feet. They drank carefully because there was a camp restriction forbidding the use of liquor. Except for the orange glow of other fires, the camp was dark. Smoke and tiny red cinders, the noise of scattered conversations, occasional laughter, and the music from a single harmonica drifted into their eyes and ears. On the other side of the river, the monuments and buildings of the nation's capital glowed brightly like the Land of Oz.

Although Emma rarely touched alcoholic beverages, she took a couple of sips. She didn't like the taste, but the whisky helped ease her body's pains. Her thoughts drifted back in time, cataloging the scenes of their travels from Mystic Heights in the year 2032 to Washington, D.C., in 1932. It was just a few days, but it seemed they had been here forever. She winced at the thought of that man attacking her on the train, and she could not get the image out of her head. Waves of strange feelings crashed against a wall of denial, mixed with the warmth of the cheap whisky, and receded. She relived the disturbing events in the light and sounds of the crackling fire under the sleepy clouds and the half-moon above. Somehow, not all of her thoughts were laden with fear or dressed in evil; instead, some of her memories of that terrible experience made her feel alive as she had never felt before. These emotions mystified her. Then, in response to someone's comment, a strong voice erupted from their circle and shook her thoughts back to the present.

Branko was making a point, and the more difficulty he

had expressing himself in English, the louder his voice became. "But why bring women and children into camp. This is no place for them. Surely there must be someplace else they could have stayed. There is danger here. Danger of all kinds. Women and children should be protected."

John Sweeny spoke. "Quiet down, please. There are eyes everywhere." He held his glass up. "And this stuff is forbidden here."

"I am sorry," muttered Branko. "But...?"

"You don't understand. Me and all these other fellows are flat broke. When we left our homes, people stole milk from doorsteps, scavenged through garbage cans, and sent their kids out to beg on the street. We don't have jobs, homes, or money. We have our women and children with us because otherwise, they would end up on the street or worse. If you think I like this, you're wrong. But I don't have a choice. Anyway, when we get our bonus money, things will change."

"Thought that was dead, John," said Ethan. "Congress is out of town for the next few months. You will all be leaving soon. Right?"

"That's not true. Just two nights ago, we had seventeen thousand men surrounding the Capitol. They know we mean business. Hoover should spend some time with his two chickens stewing in his pot. But he left town, along with the chickens in Congress. He ignores us. Pretends we're not here. But General Butler will be here tomorrow," he said, raising his voice, then lowering it again. "He'll get us going again. He's a soldier's soldier. General Smedley Darlington Butler. Damn. You'll see. You'll see."

Over the top of her glass, Emma gazed at Zak. He seemed to study the moon with little interest in the campfire conversation. Finally, he looked back and noticed her. He smiled and signed, *"Beautiful night for romance or riots, isn't it?"*

LOG of Zak Newman

July 18, 1932 (local time): 21:00 (Day 6 of time travel)

Mucking out latrines is not my idea of fun. Or, for that matter, progress. But I guess someone has to do it. We busted our tails today. And our new friend Branko has proved to be a hard worker. He seems like a reasonable guy. While doing the wonderful mucking out, Ethan and I tried to get him to open up. But he didn't tell us too much about his former circus lifestyle. He simply said he was from Serbia and he used to be a very successful performer on the trapeze. Apparently, he left Europe for America in October 1929. Very auspicious timing. When he arrived in this country, it was in the grips of the great stock market crash. He told us he had no interest in getting another circus gig. He wanted to start a new life here and do something completely different. So I guess he got his wish. For the past couple of years, he's been knocking around doing odd jobs and just trying to make things work. He seems like a sad fellow. But he also has great affection and concern for Emma. When he talks about our Emma, his words almost seem fatherly.

Emma seems different since her horrible experience on the train. I don't blame her. It was nasty, and we did put her in harm's way. I wonder what's on her mind. Tonight, when we were talking alone after dinner, she mentioned that somehow she felt abandoned. When I attempted to counter this, she acknowledged that Ethan and I were always in her corner, that we would always be there. But somehow, I could tell that something was different inside of her. Something that she wouldn't reveal to her old friend Zak or to her brother. Something very personal has captured her mind and spirit.

Another strange item, she mentioned that when she was cleaning the Sweeny's hovel, she accidentally knocked over a shoe box that emptied on the ground — out fell old photos, war medals, dog tags, and something that looked to her like a grenade. It was solid metal, about the size and shape of a pear, colored army green, and had a molded checkerboard surface. She said she had seen this type of thing in many war movies over the years, and she's certain that it's an explosive weapon. Probably something left over from the World War. She told no one but Ethan and me. I don't know what to make of this, but it just shows the dangerous underbelly of this mass of men.

Tomorrow we are expecting the arrival of General Butler. We did our homework on this fellow before leaving. He's quite a renegade in history. All in all, it should be quite interesting to hear what he has to say and to see how it affects all these desperate people. The scuttlebutt in camp is that the camp commander, Walter Waters, is not too thrilled with the General's impending arrival. There are other rumors that it is good fortune that Butler will arrive soon because he will reinforce the military discipline of the camp.

On the other hand, it could stir up the troops. Something that Waters desperately wants to avoid. At this moment, the Bonus Army is a threatening military division of belligerent ex-soldiers, at least in the eyes of the national government. Waters just seems to be trying to get the men to leave peacefully before trouble starts. And we know from The History…that real trouble is very near.

End 07-18-32

Chapter VII

The General

The following day broke with the sound of a thousand campsites coming to life. Pots and pans banged, coffee percolated, children cried, and dogs barked. The three time-travelers and Branko had spent their first and only night sleeping in the marcher camp. Emma found the experience enlightening but painful. Her bed for the night had been a double layer of cardboard with her jacket doubled up as a pillow. She awoke with pains in all parts of her body. The men suffered through a similar sleepless night. Everyone wondered how the marchers and their families could contend with such hardship. After a simple breakfast of oatmeal and coffee, they thanked the Sweeny family for their hospitality and went on their way. Now they would have to find other sleeping accommodations outside the camp. Commander Waters had made that quite clear. Before leaving, Emma had renewed her promise to assist Molly Sweeny as much as possible during the daytime hours.

They walked through the camp for several hours, talking with people to assess the situation. They learned there were more protesters nearby in downtown locations, maybe ten to twelve thousand additional people. Also, the Communist emplacement was located in one of these areas. The local police had required political isolation to reduce trouble. Their goal was to separate the bona fide war veterans from those who came to Washington to cause problems. Bad blood existed between the non-Communist veterans and the Communists, some of whom were veterans. Apparently, secret police patrolled the marcher camp to spot Communists. If anyone passed out seditious literature, he could be captured by the camp police, tried, and convicted on site. Removal was the minimum sentence; some were whipped. Many people in the Anacostia camp thought the Communists were simply taking advantage of the situation to promote their political agenda. The Bonus Marchers in the Anacostia camp seemed to be apolitical. They were there to get their bonus money.

After they toured the camp, Branko announced that he would visit the city's downtown areas, and after he left, the time travelers walked to the nearby Anacostia River. They sat on the bank in the shade of one of the few scruffy trees along the water. It was going to be another hot July day. Across the river, the Navy yard bustled with ship movements and dock activity. The historical tall ship *U.S.S. Constitution* lay anchored at its docks. Beyond that, the people of the city of Washington were no doubt moving slowly this morning, limiting any physical exertion under a deep layer of oppressive heat and humidity.

The warm weather released an unpleasant smell from the river that wafted off the oily surface of the water. Smells like this did not exist in the future world, thought Emma. She was more open-minded than her brother or Zak concerning the reality of the world of 1932. It certainly was primitive compared to their world of the future. And it really smelled. Not just the industrial smells but the personal odors were also somewhat disturbing. The pungent aromas emitted by the camp people often caused Zak to make faces. When he did, Emma chided him. She told him he was not much of an explorer. People smelled here. It was a feature of the human and physical landscape, just like the funny-looking old automobiles, the complete lack of air conditioning, the men wearing straw hats and spitting chewing tobacco, and the women with bad teeth and bizarre hats. Everyone smoked cigarettes or cigars, and the smoke thoroughly impregnated their clothes. Body odors oozed from clothes not washed or cleaned unless absolutely necessary. And personal deodorants had apparently not yet been put into play. The world the time travelers knew, the world of 2032, was an antiseptic, odoriferous desert compared to the world of the 1930s. It was all part of the adventure for Emma. Ethan and Zak ultimately agreed with her. This was a foreign land with unsavory smells and sights, but one having an innate, gritty excitement not even hinted at in their own time. The people of 1932 were alive, smells and all.

Zak sat on the ground and leaned with his back against the truck of the tree. Ethan and Emma stood by the river, absentmindedly tossing stones into the murky green water. There was another splash just a few feet in front of them. They were startled. Zak laughed, and they turned around.

"I had to get your attention. I can't exactly shout, you know. I asked a question. What about General Butler?"

Emma and Ethan returned and sat down next to him. "Sorry, Zak," said Emma. "We didn't mean to ignore you. Anyway...General Butler." She leaned back on her outstretched hands, allowing the full sun to hit her face. "According to Molly, General Smedley Darlington Butler is the most decorated Marine in United States history. I think he has 16 medals, including two Medals of Honor. The man is quite a soldier."

"And he's coming here today. Right?" asked Ethan.

"That's what Molly and Mr. Sweeny said. The whole camp is waiting for him with high expectations."

"He's an unusual guy," said Ethan. "He fought in wars all over the world. Cuba, the Philippines, Central America, China, France. This guy was everywhere. And you know what he is famous for saying?"

Zak shrugged.

"He said: 'War is a racket.' His view was that the rich guys used the armed forces of the United States as their personal muscle to assure that their corporate fortunes would not be taken over by hostile foreigners. He was quite blunt about this. He called himself a 'gangster for capitalism.' He retired last year. 1931. Major General."

"The Bonus Marchers love him," said Emma.

"He's no friend of President Hoover either." Ethan laughed. "Hoover put him up for court-martial, but they dropped the charges."

"What did he do to deserve that?"

"I think he bad-mouthed the Italian dictator, Mussolini."

"Sounds like my kind of guy."

"We'll see. He should be arriving soon."

General Butler stood on a raised platform. He was small and thin. Nevertheless, he had a commanding presence. In shirtsleeves, his pants held up with suspenders, his tie flapping in the breeze, his black hair disheveled, and his voice loud and raspy, the General spoke to his troops. Thousands of war veterans with their families and several newsreel cameramen surrounded the podium. His audience hung on his every word. "Old Gimlet Eye," they called him. As John Sweeny had said, he was "a soldier's soldier." Emma, Ethan, and Zak watched from a distance. Nearby, John Sweeny and his entire family stood mesmerized at the sight and sound of the old soldier. It was a short speech, made longer by the constant applause and cheering from the audience.

"I'm here because I've been a soldier for thirty-five years, and I can't resist the temptation to be among soldiers." He spoke of the righteousness of their cause and told them he was with them. He told them they were right. Finally, he delivered these lines from his heart and memory. "Usually, soldiers don't know what it is all about. Somebody beats a drum, somebody yells 'patriotism,' and the soldiers go out, carry the guns, get shot, and, when there is no war, do all the suffering at home. In peace times, they suffer, and in war times, they bleed."

"When you got ready to go to war to lick the Huns, what did you do? You first learned how to fight, and a whole lot of brass-hats wrote a lot of instructions on how to shoot, how to march, how to do everything, so that you all marched together, keeping step. You all spoke the same language. You all had the same objective, and when anybody asked you your general orders, you all said the same thing."

"I know who's made this country worth living in. It's

just you fellows. Look. Makes me so damn mad! A whole lot of people speak of you as tramps. By God, they didn't speak of you as tramps in 1917 and 1918. No." He paused. And they cheered loudly.

"Take it from me; this is the greatest demonstration of Americanism we've ever had. Pure Americanism. Willing to take this beating that you've taken, stand right steady, and keep every law. And why the hell shouldn't you? Who in the hell has done all the bleeding for this country, for this law, and for this constitution? You fellows. So don't step back. Hang together and stick it out till the gates of hell freeze over. If you don't, you are no damn good." He told them that the election in November could change things for the better. But, he also cautioned them, "Don't break any laws and don't allow people to say bad things about you. If you slip over into lawlessness of any kind, you will lose the sympathy of a hundred twenty million people in this nation."

With that, he jumped off the platform and walked into the crowd. Thousands cheered. John Sweeny hugged his wife. Their two toddlers jumped and ran around, circling their parents. And Colleen, the baby, continued to sleep as she had throughout the entire event. The throng of people spontaneously sang "Sweet Adeline" as a tribute to General Butler. Emma's eyes grew watery. It was a great speech. She was overwhelmed to be a part of history.

Then a well-dressed man standing in front of them throughout the speech turned and walked toward them. He looked at Emma. Concerned about her appearance, she dried her eyes quickly and studied the man before her. He was, by anyone's definition, quite handsome and tall. He had the bearing of someone in control, and at this moment, he had her complete attention. "Well, young lady. I see the good General has touched your heart." He smiled, exposing a tailored set of white teeth, set off by the bronze color of his suntanned face. Slowly he turned his attention to Ethan and Zak. "I'm sorry. May I introduce myself? I'm Jack Travers."

The three travelers greeted the stranger. Travers' eyes

locked onto Emma's. And when they shook hands, he held her hand in his just a moment longer than necessary. He looked at Zak and Ethan. "I couldn't help but notice you. You don't appear old enough to have fought in the World War. Maybe you have friends or relatives here?"

Emma listened and watched. Maybe it was an after-effect of the General's speech or something else, but this man excited her. He was handsome, but that was not all. He had something special. She couldn't understand her feelings at this moment. And, she desperately wished she wasn't dressed in her authentic "hobo-look" clothes. She was almost unable to talk, an unusual predicament for Emma. She stumbled to provide an answer, but the words wouldn't come out. Her brother grabbed the conversational ball and ran with it.

"We're here to help the Bonus Marchers," said Ethan. "And you?"

Travers pulled out a pack of cigarettes and offered them to the three travelers. They declined, and he lit one. Emma noticed the silver lighter bearing an insignia. Blowing out a blast of smoke downwind, he resumed his banter. "Me? I'm here on behalf of Governor Roosevelt. Just nominated and the next President of the United States...if I may be so bold." He slid his gaze over to Emma, and he smiled again. "What about you, Emma? Have you heard of Mr. Roosevelt?

She looked into his deep, dark brown eyes. There was something there that she wanted, but she didn't know what it was. Seconds passed. She regained her composure. "Of course I have. I have the greatest respect for Mr. Roosevelt and for his wife. I am pleased to know he has asked you here today." She finished the sentence and coughed.

"Sorry...should I put this out?" Travers looked concerned.

Emma shook her head gently. "No. That's not necessary. My throat must just be dry."

Travers smiled. "Maybe I can buy you a lemonade?

Whet your whistle?"

"Thanks. Maybe later," she said in an encouraging tone. "Will Mr. Roosevelt put through the bonus payment if elected?"

"Well, he is very interested in what is going on. He wants to get all the facts. I am his eyes and ears in Washington. And I must say that some of what I see here today is amazing." He gave her a quick flash of teeth and flipped his head back, almost like Franklin Roosevelt himself.

Having seen photos of the candidate in many local newspapers, Emma recognized Travers' impression. She laughed. "I see you like to imitate your boss."

It was his turn to chuckle. "You got me there, Emma. It happens to many people. If you're around the great man for any time, you soon pick up his mannerisms. A delightful fellow and his wife Eleanor is charming and brilliant."

Emma looked over to Zak, almost as if she was asking his opinion without saying anything. His expression was one of displeasure. "I get all my political advice from my friend Zak. Right, Zak?" she said in response to nothing.

Zak looked perplexed. He quickly signed, *"What the heck are you talking about?"*

While Zak replied, Emma was looking at Jack Travers. Strangely, he appeared to be following their conversation. But she did not mention this, only making a mental note of this possibility. "Zak says he would like to meet Mr. Roosevelt sometime. And so would I. As would my brother Ethan, I'm sure."

"That's why I'm here, and he's not. He needs to know what's happening around the country, and I'm sure he would like to meet you, but I don't think that will happen. At least not now. I believe Mr. Roosevelt will turn this country around. You know, we could use some bright young people like you. I will mention it to the boss. How long will you stay in Washington?"

Ethan answered, "Well, that's an excellent question. As of tonight, we have no place to stay. Commander Waters allowed us to stay one night, which I guess was a bit unusual. But our intention is to stay here and help the marchers."

Travers squinted in the bright sun. He gazed at the crowd as if he was thinking. Then he smiled. "You know, I just might be able to help you find accommodations. That is if you're not too picky."

"That's a laugh. We spent the whole day yesterday mucking out latrines. I don't think there's anything you could offer that would be worse than our accommodations last night." Zak finished signing and laughed.

Ethan and Emma chuckled. Emma translated for Travers.

"Well, I don't have any trenches to clean. I'm actually thinking of a place with running water."

Emma slid over to get closer to Travers. She'd had enough of sleeping on cardboard. It was sapping her energy. Time for some charm, she thought. She looked into his eyes and said, "That would be wonderful, Mr. Travers. Really keen. Is there a bath?"

"I think that could be arranged, Emma. And please, call me Jack."

"OK. Jack..."

"What about Branko?" asked Ethan.

"Who?"

"Branko is a friend of ours from Serbia. Have room for a fourth?"

"Well, you're a pretty demanding group. But I'm always open to helping deserving people, especially when they are as pretty as Emma."

They spent the next hour touring the camp. Jack Travers seemed quite at ease with everyone. Emma was taken by his gregarious manner. He was like a politician, she thought. Dancing from one shack to the next, talking, listening, asking questions, and all the time promoting Franklin Roosevelt. He seemed to put people at ease. These people were no friends to any politician, but Travers had a way with them. This was a man who understood people, thought Emma. Everyone seemed to like him. And she liked him, too. There was something special about this man from the moment they met. This trip was getting interesting, she thought.

Toward the end of their loop around the camp, Branko appeared. He was very animated and wanted to tell everyone about his conversations with the downtown marchers. Ethan cut the discussion short. "We've got a place to stay, Branko. You can tell us all about it later."

DATE: July 20, 1932
REPORT OF ACTIVITIES: Washington, D.C.
Bonus Marchers
FROM: Jack Travers

General Smedley Butler arrived at Camp Marks yesterday. He gave a speech before gathering the entire camp of veterans and their families. As to the concern that his presence might increase tensions or the possibility of violence, I can report that the General was very cautious in his delivery and was not a provocateur. He is very sympathetic to the cause of the Bonus Army, and while he called on them to stand firm on their demands for the issuance of a bonus, he reminded them that they were all soldiers and that they must maintain order and discipline. The men in the camp were responsive to him and his speech.

I have also noticed that the average person on the street here in Washington favors the marchers' cause. Local citizens are not concerned with keeping the national budget in check or other similar political issues that have held back the early delivery of the marchers' bonuses. The people appear to have accepted the thousands of new guests into their city with welcome arms, and they have no fear that disruptions or danger will ensue.

I have been told that General Butler stayed the night after speaking encamped with the troops and that he left this morning after delivering a brief and somber speech.

There are no signs of violence at this time. Although the

government has demanded that the marchers leave town, no enforcement measures are in evidence. The relationship between the camp leader (Commander Waters) and the local police (Chief Glassford) continues to be amicable. The camp residents continue to be assisted by local government and concerned citizens alike. Note that Mrs. McLean has interceded and secured food and shelter for some marchers. Overall, things are peaceful, but conditions are deteriorating. Daily more marchers arrive. The camp conditions are becoming almost unlivable. A young boy died of measles and pneumonia about two weeks ago. He suffered from malnutrition. Donations of meat and other foods continue to be made, but this is a city within a city filled with men, women, and children who have no money and no place to go. They remain here by inertia as much as desire. It is a challenging situation.

More men are arriving each day. Just a few blocks from the Capitol, members of the Bonus Army and the contingent of Communists occupy vacant buildings. Hundreds of veterans have been sleeping overnight on the lawns surrounding the Capitol. The massive meeting of veterans at the Capitol on July 16th was attended by 17,000.

Communist forays against the White House have stopped. However, protests occur daily in the streets. There have been minor skirmishes between the police and the marchers. The government is demanding the marchers leave. The Communists have already tried to cause trouble. And I believe they would like to use this opportunity to increase their power and create disruption. For them, violence is a political tool. However, the police have maintained order. Glassford appears to be balancing the needs of the citizens of Washington and those of the thousands of visitors. He has done a remarkable job.

President Hoover is maintaining a low profile. He has not made any public appearances, and, in fact, he did not attend the adjournment of Congress, some say, out of fear for his life. My conversations with congressional aides indicate a growing fear that either the Communists, the marchers, or the police will incite a riot. They also fear the militaristic nature of the protestors, knowing that the ex-soldiers in Washington and around the country could provide organized support for fascist elements. However, this concern appears only to be based on nervous speculation. No one has attempted to harness these forces for political advantage. But this and other factors are an indication that the situation may be moving toward a boiling point.

If I may make a recommendation, I would suggest that every effort be made to provide food and medical supplies to the occupiers through charitable sources. Hungry, desperate, and disappointed people breed violence. The authorities have offered the marchers transportation home, but few have accepted that offer. On the whole, they are staying put. The situation appears to be drifting into a deteriorating stalemate between the government and the Bonus Army.

-Chapter VIII-

Under the Decision Tree

It was time for the time travelers to make their move. Branko remained in the basement apartment that Travers had found while they headed out for a walk and a quick confab. Their new home was a former servants' quarters located on the lower floor of a large residence. A small bedroom for Emma, a larger one for the three men, a living room, a tiny kitchen, and one bathroom for everyone. It was tight but ritzy compared to the marcher camp. Travers told them this house was owned and occupied by his landlord. Somehow, the apartment was provided as a courtesy to the travelers. Travers had only smiled when asked about that aspect. When pressed, he suggested that the landlord was very partial to the Roosevelts and that affinity extended to Jack Travers and his friends. Washington dealings, thought Emma, always one hand washing the other. But she was relieved to be sleeping in a real bed instead of a cardboard facsimile. Her back ached from the sleepover at the Sweeny place.

A short walk brought them to Folger Park, which offered the luxury of benches, fresh air, greenery, and the anonymous privacy of a public place, the city block was designed as an oval promenade with a square, landscaped island in the center. In the comforting shade of a large tree, they sat side by side on one of the benches facing the world.

"*L'Enfant*," signed Zak.

"The baby?" asked Ethan.

"No, the city plan. This park must be based on the work of the architect L'Enfant. Diagonals, ovals, circles, and a grid. Just like the whole city. Versailles gardens on steroids. Very pretty."

"Also, good for moving troops around," said Ethan.

Emma was not listening to their conversation but thinking about her upcoming afternoon with Jack Travers. A couple of days ago, at General Butler's rally, the handsome Washington insider offered to buy her lemonade, and today he was going to stop by to make good on his offer. He wanted to "show her the town." She was interested in the tour, but she had her own agenda. In her mind, Travers could be the key to the entire history-shaking situation that the time travelers wanted to massage for the better.

"Enjoying the view?" asked Ethan.

Emma snapped out of her trance. She coughed.

"Still have that nasty cough...."

"Yes, I do. I must be allergic to something. Maybe mold. Heat and humidity create mold. And Camp Marks is filled with mud."

"My nose has been running like a faucet," said Ethan. "Has to be allergies. We're not used to the massive pollen and mold count here."

"I could hardly sleep with all the noise coming out of your room last night," signed Zak.

"Right," she said. "I can't imagine you bothered by anything. You can sleep anywhere. You slept like a baby riding in those boxcars."

"L'enfant de chemin de fer," Zak spoke silently with his hands and laughed, apparently quite pleased with this attempt at Euro-humor.

"Baby Zak. Goo, goo," said Ethan.

"Anda a bañarte," replied Zak.

"Boys..."

"OK," said Ethan. "What about the massacre? Let's talk strategy. Let's plan. Let's get something going here. A week from today, this town is going to explode, and the presidential election is going down the tubes. We've got the old needle in the haystack. We know that the massacre is coming, and we know that the Communists are the cause...."

Emma interrupted. "If you believe *The History*, there was some kind of major disturbance on July 28, 1932.

And we know that whatever it was, it led to retaliation by the Army. Troops fired on the crowd. Marchers died. And a riot ensued. More people died. And then, in response, all across the nation, people rose up against the government. Communists, veterans, the unemployed."

"*And then martial law was declared,*" said Zak. "*El final.*"

"That is *correctomundo*, my friend," said Ethan. "And that is why we are going to attack this problem at its source...the Communists. They're the ones who started it. You can see yourself that the marchers are a well-behaved and controlled group. But the Communists...they're looking for trouble, according to Branko. Before going to sleep last night, Zak and I talked with him for quite a while. He said when he went downtown to the Communist camp, he spoke directly to the leader of the group. A guy named Pace. According to Branko, this is the guy who led the moonlight march on the White House just before we arrived here. Scared the heck out of President Hoover. Pace and his men will push the police as far as possible. Soon...according to Branko."

Zak moved to a new position, sitting on the back of the bench. "Branko can get us near the inner circle of Communists. He seems tight with them. And somehow, someplace, they're going to be involved."

Emma wondered about her protector, Branko. Was he involved with the Communists? If not, why was he so interested in them? She trusted him, but she didn't know where he stood except that he seemed very concerned about the welfare of the vets and their families. "Maybe Branko can help. *The History* blames it all on the Communists. But even if it's right for once, why should we wait to perform some last-minute magic? You know that didn't work out with President Kennedy. The only thing we accomplished was to get a ringside view of the whole horrific thing."

"Not so, Emma. You forget we did save JFK once."

"I remember. And remember, I'm the one who worked the deal. But ultimately, that didn't really help him stay in office. Unfortunately, he moved into martyrdom. We've got a similar situation here. Soon many people will die, and the country will slide quickly into martial law and fascism. We've got to get ahead of this one, guys. And I have an idea."

"Yes. Yes. Go ahead, *El Supremo*," said Ethan.

Emma smirked. "Jack Travers may be our ticket out of trouble. The man has Roosevelt's ear. You heard him. If we can just get him to influence the Governor to arrange to pay the marchers their bonus...."

Ethan scratched the back of his head and wore a dubious look. "Hey. You're talking about two billion dollars. That's billion with a 'B.' Big money in 1932. Where's that coming from?"

"I'm not sure," she said. "But if he could just make it one of his campaign promises...then the government could pay it out. Remember, the House of Representatives approved the payment. So it can't be crazy money."

"But wouldn't they accuse Roosevelt of buying votes with taxpayer money?" asked Zak.

"And your point is?" She shook her head. "Isn't that what politicians do? Just think, if Mr. Roosevelt declared this publicly, he could ask the marchers to show good faith by leaving town. If they leave town before the Army attacks, no one gets hurt. I think it is worth the gamble. If he doesn't do something...or if we aren't able to stop the violence...then he has no chance to win the election. Because there will be no presidential election. Right?"

Ethan looked at Zak, and both shrugged their shoulders and nodded. "But remember, Roosevelt doesn't know the future like we do. He's going to base his decisions on the assumption that the election is on," said Ethan. "You're going to meet with your new buddy Jack anyway. So go ahead. See what you can accomplish. Zak and I will work the Branko angle. We're heading downtown to meet up with him now."

"Be careful, guys...promise?" said Emma.

"Yes, mother," answered Ethan.

They both laughed and sauntered away. Masters of

time and space, she thought. She rolled her eyes skyward as if seeking divine guidance. Then, alone, she strolled through the park contemplating the entire scenario. Time was evaporating. She confirmed today's date in her mind. It was the 21st. One week remained until America changed forever, or didn't.

Chapter IX

A New Hat

Earlier, though without explanation, she had informed Molly Sweeny that she could not help her today. She promised to return to the camp, but not until tomorrow. Today was dedicated to Mr. Travers.

On her way back to the apartment, she walked along a narrow street filled with small, intriguing shops. Unlike other parts of the city she had visited, this shopping street bore no signs of the Depression. There were no vacant stores, no beggars, or apple vendors on the street corners. There were no long lines of ragged men waiting for a bite to eat or a night's shelter. This part of town was upscale and affluent. Obviously, some people in Washington were not affected by the times. For them, this area offered the latest in fashion and panache. Emma moved from shop to shop, admiring the newest shoes, gowns, and swimwear. She loved the romance built into the apparel. A woman could be a woman in 1932, she thought. The window displays of one tiny French boutique caught her eye. She looked at the mannequins dressed for the summer and assessed the possibilities. She wanted to look good for Jack and had the money to buy what she needed. That part of their plan worked well. On their way out of 2032, the time travelers had "borrowed" some gold coins from Dr. Currant's collection. Emma knew he would be upset if he discovered the loss, but she thought that was the price of fixing history. Immediately upon arriving in Mystic Heights in 1932, they had visited a downtown bank and traded some of the coins for cash. The banker had appeared pleased to make the transaction, as were they. Having authentic currency was a necessity for time travelers.

She entered the store and shopped at a leisurely pace,

exploring and analyzing the clothing as if it were in a museum exhibit, comfortable with the thought that she could buy fashions that fit the time: a couple of dresses, a blouse, two hats, silk stockings, and even some authentic and provocative imported underwear. Lastly, she purchased some cosmetics. Fortunately, she had anticipated the need for dress shoes. Before they left, she had packed two pairs that she hoped would fit the times. She didn't have a choice because she assumed she would never find her size. Looking over the array of shoes on display, she knew her previous selections would work. She also confirmed that locating size 11 shoes in 1932 would be as improbable as finding a legitimate platinum blonde.

All of her purchases were put to good effect by the time Jack arrived, precisely on time. Emma was impressed with his punctuality. And she was ready. A last-minute check in the mirror proved satisfying. Her soft yellow dress and matching wide-brimmed straw hat highlighted her green eyes, showed off her figure, and contrasted neatly with her recently acquired tan. Travers continued to knock at the door of their apartment. When she answered and swept open the door, it was like the curtain coming up on a stage. Travers seemed astonished, and she was somewhat taken aback by his reaction. Apparently, the transformation from their last meeting to today, from the hobo girl wearing overalls and a lumberjack shirt to someone quite a bit more sophisticated, was a resounding success. For a moment, they just looked at each other.

"Say, you look swell, Emma," he said. "Better than swell. You're quite a dish. If you'll pardon the expression."

"Flattery will get you everywhere, Jack Travers." She smiled. "Well, I did some shopping today. I didn't want you to be embarrassed."

"Quite the opposite, my dear. Heads will be turning. You ready?"

"I am," she said, her voice betraying her excitement.

They went places that clear, hot July afternoon. Jack

drove an open roadster, ivory and dark brown and very stylish. Although intrigued, Emma did not ask him about it. He was obviously a man who had things or was able to get them when he wanted. Her hair tossed about in the wind as they wheeled in and out of the light late-afternoon Washington traffic. The monument tour included a drive by the Capitol building. That area was filled with people. The marchers were preparing for their continuous "death march," as they called it, a nonstop moving picket of marching veterans holding signs and American flags. They sang as they marched, probably as they did during the war; only now the villain in the songs was not the Kaiser but rather President Hoover.

They drove past rows of abandoned four-story warehouse buildings. Some were partially demolished. The exterior walls had been peeled away, revealing the vets' living quarters, open air, with total exposure and no privacy. Peering into these oversized doughboy dollhouses was like looking into the soul of the marcher movement. Sad, she thought. The reality of this place was no better than the other camp on the Anacostia: city mice versus country mice, scurrying around looking for scraps. Only the military discipline these men had acquired in wartime allowed the potential chaos to be organized and held in check. But here, the possibility of an explosion of violence seemed even more likely than at Camp Marks. These people were stuffed and stacked into their makeshift quarters four stories high.

"This is called Camp Glassford," Jack shouted above the wind and noise of the convertible. "Named after the chief of police. This whole area houses veterans. They live in these old government buildings. Maybe ten thousand of them. Glassford found this shelter for them, and they rewarded him with the name. But now I understand the President wants them out. Soon."

"Why do they call the one on the river Camp Marks?" she asked.

"Named after the head cop in that area. Another good guy, or so I hear."

"Are the Communists located here?"

"What?"

"The 'reds'...are they here?"

"Yes. They're in one of these buildings. But there are only a few hundred of them. A small but troublesome bunch."

Emma thought about her brother, Zak, and Branko. They might be nearby. What were they doing? That thought was quickly lost as Jack skillfully motored out of the area. Soon they were out of the confines of the city, traveling on the winding road that followed the Potomac River. For a few minutes, the entire world fell away for Emma. She was twenty-one years old and free. She basked in the sun, hand atop her hat against the wind, like a Hollywood starlet riding in an open-top car with her handsome, intelligent leading man admiring her at every opportunity. And he was admiring her. The only thing about him that bothered her was that he smoked cigarettes. Earlier, she had asked him to refrain from doing so because it aggravated her cough. Without hesitation, he agreed to stop. He told her he had only started smoking recently and didn't like the habit anyway. Non-smoking was something he would work on for her. His comment pleased her very much.

The road curved to the left, at once exposing the massive monument. "There it is, Emma. The Lincoln Memorial," said Jack.

Emma was impressed. The white marble colonnaded building seemed to float on the green grass and blue sky horizon. "An American acropolis. The Parthenon on the Potomac. Mr. Lincoln would be proud."

Jack laughed. "I don't know. He was born in a log cabin. This might be a little rich for his tastes."

"Maybe you're right. But Lincoln was a man of the people. Like your Mr. Roosevelt."

Travers flipped his head back again, *à la* his boss. "Too soon to tell, my dear. I was born in a cabin of marble and gold. Not a log in sight. But let the people decide. I am just their humble servant," he said, giving his best impression of Roosevelt.

"Was that him again?"

"Sorry," said Jack. "I can't resist. He is infectious. In a good way."

"Well, I hope he becomes the next president, and I know it can happen."

Jack gave her a quizzical look. She smiled knowingly.

Travers parked the car, and they strolled up to the structure. Their hands bumped against each other, and Emma wished he would hold her hand. But that didn't happen. They spent time inside the building visiting the giant statue seated in an oversized chair and admiring the view of the Washington Monument at the terminus of the mall reflecting pool. They listened to the tour guide tell the tale of the 16th president: his rise to prominence from humble beginnings, his struggles in the Civil War, and in some detail, his assassination in 1865.

Emma was saddened by this retelling of history. Lincoln had his Grecian temple, and Kennedy had his tiny eternal flame, but not forever. JFK's glimmer of remembrance was extinguished sometime in the 2020s. The city was abandoned and moved to a safer desert location. Imposing empty buildings deteriorated and became historical artifacts like the ancient ruins of Europe. As she absorbed the tour guide's description of Lincoln's demise, the words took her back to Dallas, Texas, in 1963, when she witnessed the death of another president. Emotion overcame her, and memories melted into tears that she could not stifle. Jack Travers sensed her distress. Quickly, he escorted her outside the building. They walked around the back and sat on a stone bench in a quiet area facing the river. Emma stared out vacantly. Jack gave her his handkerchief, and she dried her tears.

He held her hand. A flood of new emotions filled her being. Whether this was massive sorrow or immense joy, she did not know. At this moment, she really had no thoughts, only emotion.

Head down, she mumbled the words. "Oh. I am so

sorry."

"What is it, my dear?" He moved closer. His body was up against hers; his face was near. He looked into her eyes. Everything meshed into oneness with him. She brought her body tight to his and rested her head on his shoulder. She sobbed and coughed, then gently pulled away to blow her nose into his silk handkerchief.

She shook her head. "I'm sorry."

He laughed. "I guess that is what it is for. It's been waiting in my pocket just for this occasion." He pulled out a silver whisky flask from his jacket pocket. "Here. Have a drink."

"No. No, thanks."

"It will help," he said quietly.

She sipped, then coughed, then smiled. In a moment, she felt the effects of the drink. "Better," she said. "I can explain, Jack," she muttered.

"You don't have to, Emma." He held her hand again.

"No. I must." She paused to think. "I once knew a man who touched me deeply, but he died. Sadly, he died right before my eyes. I don't know. I was overcome just now with the talk of President Lincoln's death. It's so stupid."

"I don't think honest emotion is ever stupid, Emma. I think it can be beautiful. And I think you are beautiful."

As his words entered the foggy void of her mind, she pulled him toward her slowly and deliberately until their lips met in a kiss of passion, love, romance, and a thousand other nuances. Emma was overwhelmed with an intense explosion of vibrations, unlike anything she had ever experienced in her entire life. At that moment, she and Jack were one.

Emma was giddy as they drove back to her apartment. Jack had turned on the radio. Bing Crosby sang "Out of Nowhere." It was as if he sang only to her that late afternoon in Washington, D.C., in 1932. The music caressed her mind as she looked at Jack. What a remarkable man. He glanced at her, and she smiled. For her, it was a delightful moment to be savored. No one had ever been this close to her. Aside from the romantic qualities of her new relationship with Jack, which she knew little but enjoyed very much, she was also aware that she and Jack were connecting. They had quickly become friends and confidants. Although not planned, it was precisely the situation that Emma would want. Since time was of the essence, she decided to jump right in.

Jack pulled the roadster to a neat stop in front of her building. Late afternoon sunlight cast long shadows across the tree-lined street. A woman walking by glanced at the handsome man and the pretty young woman. She smiled at Jack, but he did not respond. Instead, he turned to face Emma and casually rested his arm on the top of the seat, his fingers toying with her hair.

"Did you have fun today, Emma?"

"I loved every minute of it." She rolled her eyes. "Well, almost every minute. But..."

"But what?"

"But I have to talk to you about something. It's important."

"Go on..."

"I want to talk with you about this situation with the marchers. I know you're here to report back to the Governor. But we can do so much more than that. I believe that Mr. Roosevelt has the power to defuse this entire dangerous situation."

Jack laughed. "Emma. You are a delightful person. Kind-hearted, intelligent, and beautiful. But please leave the politics to the experts."

Emma lost her smile. "You haven't heard me out, Jack."

He retreated. "OK. Sorry. You're right. What's on your mind?"

"I would like to meet with Mr. Roosevelt. I want to discuss the idea of him promising to pay out the veterans' bonus money."

Travers shrugged his shoulders. "Emma, even Mr. Roosevelt doesn't have that kind of money."

"Right. That I know. But he could promise the

marchers that, if he is elected, he will do everything in his power to have Congress pass the bill to release the funds. If the marchers knew this, they might leave Washington and vote for Governor Roosevelt in November."

"You're really concerned about these people, aren't you?"

"Yes. I am. I think at this moment, Washington is a powder keg ready to explode."

"Sorry, but I know Mr. Roosevelt won't take a stand on this issue. It's too obvious and too dangerous to promise anything to anyone. This is Hoover's problem, and the smart political decision now is to do nothing."

Emma's frustration was building. "Not smart, Jack. Expedient. Something must be done."

"Sounds like you have inside information," said Jack as he removed his arm from the seat back.

"I've worked inside the camp. I sense their pain. I was with the Sweeny family yesterday. They live under terrible conditions, and they have nowhere else to go. Their backs are up against the wall. And our friend Branko has met with some of the Communists. They're not kidding, Jack. They want blood in the streets. And, also, I would guess that President Hoover is at the end of his rope."

Jack put both hands on the steering wheel. He gazed out the windshield before turning back to face her. "I can see you are serious about this, Emma. But you'll have to forget about meeting with Mr. Roosevelt. I've been working for him for over a year, and you know how many times I've met with him?"

"Tell me."

"I will. The answer is once. When I was hired. So I am certain you and I are not going to discuss anything with him because neither of us will get an audience."

Emma puckered her lips.

He looked at her carefully. "You getting ready to kiss me?" he asked.

"No, I am not. Shhh...I'm thinking." She remained quiet. "How do you communicate with him if you never meet?"

"That is the trick, my dear. That is the trick. I communicate with Mrs. Roosevelt, and she with me. Mostly by letter or memo. Sometimes by telegram or telephone. Very rarely in person. She is my link to the Governor; I would say she is not just a messenger for him. He places high value on her advice, opinion, and direction. They have a very unusual but strong relationship."

Emma puckered again and erupted into speech. "That's it, Jack...."

He moved closer to her and put his arm around her shoulders. "You know, you are an interesting woman."

"Jack. I want to meet with Mrs. Roosevelt. Can you make it happen?"

He nodded wisely and shrugged his shoulders. After a few seconds of contemplation, he said, "I suppose anything is possible. But what's in it for me?"

"Well, Jack," she said, thinking all time. The words created a very open, inviting smile, which she maintained for effect. "As you say, I suppose anything is possible. I need your help, Jack." His reaction was immediate and astounding. She knew she was playing some kind of word game. She was good at such banter. But she had never played the game in this arena, with a real man hanging on her every word: thinking thoughts, interpreting, interpolating, and speculating. She sensed her response was expanding in Jack Travers' mind and body, moving in directions unknown to her. She also felt a power in herself that she did not know existed until now.

He placed his hand on her leg just above her knee and, in a playful manner, squeezed it gently, sliding it up her leg a few inches before it departed and joined his other hand, cupping her face. He looked into her eyes and then kissed her quickly, darting his tongue into her mouth and backing away, leaving her surprised and aroused.

He slid back to the driver's seat. He stretched his legs and arched his body while holding the wheel as if releasing something inside. "You are in luck, Emma. I am scheduled to meet with Mrs. Roosevelt soon. I'll see if we can arrange a meeting. Who knows?"

"When?" asked Emma. "When is soon?"

"Monday, the 25th."

She expressed her thoughts aloud in a drifting voice. "I suppose that will work." Three days might be enough time. We can hope, she thought.

"I hope so," said Jack, wearing a wry smile. "Let's go to the picture show tomorrow. There's a new Pat O'Brien motion picture. It's a talkie. Do you like the movies?"

"Love them. I just love them."

"Great. Then we're on," he said. "It's a date."

"I have to help the Sweeny family in the morning, Jack. I promised."

Travers looked concerned. "I'd like you to stay away from the camp, Emma. It's too dangerous for you."

"Jack. The world is a dangerous place, but I'm a big girl."

"Your decision, Emma. But I wanted you to know of my concern. Then Saturday will work?"

"Sunday will work. If that's OK with you. Mrs. Sweeny needs the help, and I promised to give her a hand for a couple of days. She needs a break."

"Mrs. Roosevelt would be proud of you," he said. "We'll have lunch and then catch a matinee on Sunday. I'll stop by at noon." He leaned over and kissed her lightly on the cheek.

"Sunday," she said as she opened the car door. She smiled. "I'm looking forward to it."

"Wait, I'll walk you to your door," he said.

"Thanks," she replied, unaccustomed to the little courtesies of the time, "but I'm fine without you." He appeared disarmed, possibly offended by her response. She looked into his eyes. "I'll miss you, Jack. Until then."

-Chapter X-

Seeing Reds

"*A thin man, thick with thoughts*," said Zak. His conversation with Ethan played out in sign language, hands beneath the table, unheard by the others. The two time travelers sat next to each other at the end of a rough-hewn table alongside Branko. Nine other men sat at the table. The fifth-floor, open-air location atop the roof of one of Camp Glassford's abandoned warehouses offered a sparkling view of the city. Ethan digested his hamburger and milkshake lunch like a lazy lizard basking in the sun. It was all so peaceful; he almost forgot that he was in the middle of the Great Depression, one of the worst times in American history and that he was surrounded by Communists. The view was great, but the featured speaker was tiring. For the past twenty minutes, John Pace, seated at the other end of the table, had droned on. While he spoke, the time travelers maintained a silent running commentary, criticizing the orator. Branko, who had arranged for their presence at this table, tried to ignore their surreptitious verbal finger-painting. Throughout the talk, he maintained a schoolteacher's face of disapproval directed at the two, obviously hoping they would curtail their concealed conversation.

Abruptly, Pace stopped talking and looked directly at Ethan. "Am I boring you two with my information? Or are you just amusing or abusing yourselves over there? You seem agitated."

Ethan looked up, knowing he was in the limelight now. Every man at the table had his eyes focused on him. These were jobless men, black and white, serious people with no use for any shenanigans. Ethan glanced over to Zak, giving him a look of disgust. Quickly, he turned back to the speaker. "Sorry, Mr. Pace. Zak and I picked up a few body critters in our stay at Camp Marks. Bedbugs. Cooties. Something like that. They're pretty uncomfortable."

Pace was stone-faced. Then he laughed. "College boys," he said. The other men at the table also laughed. Even Branko seemed to find humor in the Communist leader's words. "I suppose life on the road is not quite as luxurious as living in a nice cozy dormitory. Well, get used to it, fellows. This is reality in America. Bug bites and all. Focus on the cause, and forget your personal issues. In time, you will master the art of disciplined living. You've been living the soft, degenerate life of the bourgeois capitalists. That's over. You don't have a job. But no one here has work. That's why we are here. The old system is broke. We all need a nice hot cleansing shower of logical, useable contemporary political ideology to eliminate the systemic vermin that is destroying our lives. You've come to the right place, gentlemen. But this is no walk in the park...understand?"

Ethan and Zak just nodded knowingly.

"Fine." Pace continued his monologue as if he had never been interrupted. "Violence is an American institution. Ask the Indians about the methods of political indoctrination used to destroy them over a period of 200 years. At least they fought the system. Americans today hang onto the debauched nightmare of the 1920s. If those days symbolized the American Dream, it is time for everyone to wake up and smell the coffee. Last March 7th, I was in Detroit. The 'motor capital' of the world. The economic Eden of the 20th century. 'River Rouge,' they call it, quite appropriately. That day, the river ran red with the blood of impoverished Americans who were shot dead by capitalist goons." He paused.

"Why? Why were these people killed? What was their crime? Well, I'll tell you. Their crime was that they were hungry. That they had no medical care. That they were unemployed. Some were Negroes disenfranchised by the system. Those good men were always the last to be hired and the first to be laid off. There were 5,000 marchers that day. Comrades. We were strong. We carried signs that read *Tax the Rich. Feed the Poor.* We marched peacefully. Then they fired upon us with machine guns. That day, Henry Ford's private army shot and killed innocent people. And he got away with it."

Pace stood up and grabbed the edge of the tabletop with both hands. "This is the beginning, gentlemen. You are the true patriots of these times. If we do not stand up for 'we the people,' who will? This country is on the knife-edge of becoming a police state run by fascist thugs. America is not unlike Germany and Italy. It is not immune from this kind of corruption. It is not an island of democracy in a blackened sea of corporate elitism. It is now, but a floundering ship of state, taking on water."

"However, we have a choice. We are here in the nation's capital for a reason. We have joined with these veterans of the 'war to end all wars' to put an end to the massive misery that has swept through America like a plague of destructive locusts. Half of our children do not have adequate food, shelter, or medical aid. People are eating dandelions and grass to stay alive. Our farmers can't make a living, and they are giving up. Twenty-five percent of the workforce is unemployed. Half of all the men in Cleveland are out of work. Homeless men ride the rails without destination and without hope, millions of lost souls."

He pounded his fist on the table. "And what about the big boys? How are they doing? Well, I'll tell you. They're making fistfuls of dollars. You won't see Henry Ford, Rockefeller, or Mellon in the breadlines. They're too busy counting their money. They have it all, gentlemen. And what do we have? We have our integrity. We have righteousness. We have the tools to remake our lives. Is it going to be easy? No. But nothing is easy. Will it be a walk in the park? No. Look at Detroit last March. That's what we're up against. These people only understand one thing. And that is power. But who has the power? Who really has the power? I'll give you the answer to that one. We do. We the people."

He sat down again. Beads of sweat appeared on his forehead. He wiped his brow with his handkerchief and continued on more quietly now. "This moment in time is our opportunity. There are twenty-five thousand angry men in town. Maybe next week there will be fifty thousand. They come from all across the nation. They come here to express their frustration with the system. But they don't know what they are doing. They were soldiers fifteen years ago. They're accustomed to taking orders. They need direction. That is what we will provide." He opened his hands before him inclusively and used them for emphasis. "That is our role. We have the answer to their one basic question. We can show them how to live. How to find happiness. And how to work together to remove all workers from the monetary morass created by a rich, carnivorous, and deceitful power structure. That is our cause. That is what we fight for. That is our only mission here in Washington. Let us proceed."

With that, he leaned back in his chair. The men gathered before him spontaneously applauded. Zak and Ethan joined in the adulation, and John Pace looked satisfied. After waiting for his followers' applause to subside, he stood and said, "It's time to get to work, comrades."

Everyone rose and quickly disbursed except for the time travelers, Branko and Pace. Pace approached the three. "Well, gentlemen, you can see what we are up to. More interesting than cleaning latrines. Wouldn't you agree?"

"A great deal more, Mr. Pace. But how can we help?" Ethan sounded quite upbeat.

"You will proceed according to the directions of your friend Mr. Branko. He will be your only contact with me from this point forward. Is that understood?"

"All right. We understand. Right, Zak?"

Zak nodded.

"Fine," said Pace. "Now, if you will, please permit Mr. Branko and me to be alone...."

Ethan looked at Zak, and they shrugged their

shoulders. They shook hands with Pace and Branko.

"OK. We'll see you back at the apartment, Branko," said Ethan. It was more of a question than a statement.

"That is correct, Ethan. Goodbye." Branko didn't smile. But that was nothing new.

Ethan gave him a goodbye thumbs-up.

"I am sorry, Ethan. What is that?"

Ethan looked at his thumb. "Oh, this." He gave him the thumbs-up again. "It's American Sign Language. It means everything is good."

This time Branko managed a smile. "I am understanding." He put his thumb in the air and waggled it. "My being American is much better now."

Pace seemed amused. "One more thing," said Pace.

Ethan and Zak both were attentive.

"Don't let the bedbugs bite."

Zak rolled his eyes. But Ethan returned the smile, and they walked away from the "red menace."

After the time travelers had left, Branko and Pace returned to the table and sat next to each other, bowed heads and voices low. They talked for the better part of an hour, with Pace and the Serbian exchanging "war stories" and Pace issuing directives. Branko enjoyed the respect he was receiving from John Pace. After all, this was the same man who led the midnight march against the White House, scaring the president into leaving town. If the Communists were to guide the masses into rebellion this July 1932, John Pace would be the man to lead the charge. So far, both men had kept their cards close to their chests. Pace really didn't seem to trust anyone, and Branko was a foreigner who still had some trouble with the nuances of the language and customs.

America was not at all like his native Serbia. His homeland was a contentious place, but the conflicting parties were easily identified by their geographic origins: Croats, Serbians, and Slovenes. The United States presented a more complex palette of politics. Alexander, the current king of Branko's home country, had turned it into a dictatorial monarchy, intending to erase the differences between peoples within his newly named country of Yugoslavia. He had banned regional flags and the idea of communism. However, Branko had retained his membership card in the Communist Party, which he had received many years ago. Branko sensed that Mr. Pace was a different kind of Communist and could not understand the complexities and positions of the Communists in Yugoslavia. Likewise, Branko found it challenging to understand the direction and function of the American Communist Party. To him, the Soviet-style concept of a people's revolution seemed outside the realm of possibility here in America. Yet, that possibility apparently appeared an attainable goal to party members in America and a real threat to the average American and those in government who feared the Communist movement. Such posturing under the banner of capitalism or communism was just that. The world's reality was a far more subtle and complex system than either group could define with their supposed opposing ideologies.

Nevertheless, he was pleased that he had retained his membership card, for it was sound currency in these quarters. Pace was right about one thing, power was the key. Ideology was the story told, but power ruled the world.

LOG of Zak Newman

July 21, 1932 (local time): 23:37 (Day 9 of time travel)

It's late, and everyone else is sleeping. To see, I'm writing under my blanket using a flashlight, or electric torch, as they are called at this time. Both Branko and Ethan are noisy sleepers, and Branko is very active at night. He must be having nightmares about something. While sleeping, he will reach out as if he's grabbing something or maybe defending himself, with loud mumbling and thrashing. Something is bothering him. On the other hand, other than his sniffling, Ethan sleeps like a big baby.

Well, things are proceeding slowly. We still don't have a clue as to what caused the riot leading to the massacre. Of course, we know the date — late in the day on the 28th of July. But that's it. And, of course, the Communists are to blame. But that indictment is almost universal. In 1932, it seems like the Communists are responsible for every disruption to the system. They are the poster boys of blame when comes to riots, mob action, and civil disturbance. Got a problem? Blame it on the "reds." So it is not surprising that The History puts the responsibility for the Bonus Massacre on them. It's like saying, "the devil made me do it." As far as I can tell, there aren't that many of them in town (maybe two or three hundred) as opposed to tens of thousands of marcher veterans and their families. But maybe the "reds" are like a grain of sand in an oyster. Maybe their irritating presence will create a revolutionary and explosive "pearl." They did get a rise out of President Hoover when they picketed the White House.

In any event, Branko is our inside man with the commies. We take our orders from him, according to Pace. So far...he has issued no orders to Junior Agents Zak or Ethan. But we stand ready for action. Branko is a man who likes to have things just his way. He doesn't say much, but when he does, it is never a request. The man gives orders. Maybe that's why Pace likes him. Branko must have sold himself well to the Communists because he is a front-liner now. I can't figure out whether he is really working for them or whether he has other plans. To stop the massacre, we will need a good bit of luck. At least if the Communists really are the cause, we are near the action. If not, we have Plan B: Emma and the mysterious Mr. Roosevelt. She was quiet about her "date" with her new friend Jack Travers. But I know she truly believes she can nip things in the bud and channel the tide of history to a peaceful resolution. Let's see. She has to convince Travers to convince Roosevelt to publicly promise to assist the veterans if and when he gets into office.

Emma is a pretty woman, and Travers seems to be all man. If that's the game she is trying to play, I think she is overmatched. Looks to me like the women of the 1930s are pretty savvy in ways that Emma knows nothing about. She is very smart, but like all the young adults of 2032, she knows little about men/women relations. With government population control vested in the IRA (Independent Reproduction Agency), average women are not in the business of baby production. This has resulted in the social neutralization of the male/female dynamic. The plots of the old "love story" movies that so fascinate Emma appear somewhat ridiculous in our world of 2032. "Buddy-movies" — male-male, female-female, male-female — are a staple of today's movie producers. But romance between different or same sexes — not really. Sure, sex happens between consenting adults, but that activity is not the result of some kind of romantic mating activity. Speaking only for myself with regard to the world of sex — yes, it happens. But with Emma, I can't say, but I would guess she's no expert on that subject. On the other hand, she has seen so many movies about love and romance that she probably remembers the appropriate lines. Who knows? Maybe she can act her way into the hearts and minds of the men — and perhaps women — of 1932. Our 2032 history books have limited utility in general, and I'm certain there was nothing useful about love, sex, and romance in those tomes. Good luck, Emma. But Ethan and I will work with the Communists and topics like "world domination" that we can understand. Love and romance — please...

End 07-21-32

-Chapter XI-

Quid Pro Quo

Today was Sunday. Traditionally, almost every shop,
store, and office was closed, but the movie theaters
remained open. The Avalon Theater, located in the Chevy
Chase area of Washington, fit Emma perfectly. Filled with
the people and atmosphere of the time, bristling with the
newness of "talking pictures" amidst an architectural
celebration reminiscent of the glorious meeting halls of
old, it was just as she imagined it. As the house lights
dimmed, Emma's excitement rose. The tinny sound of the
opening music stirred something inside her. She reached
over and held Jack Travers' hand.

He looked at her and whispered, "You look like a kid
in a candy store."

She nodded and smiled. The curtains parted, and the
credits rolled for the black-and-white flick *Hell's House*,
starring Pat O'Brien, Bette Davis, and a host of early
1930s character actors. This was a dream come true for
Emma, a true movie buff. Not that the movie was that
good. She had seen it before, but never in context. It was
1932. The Great Depression did cover the nation like a
smelly, wet blanket. Bootlegging was still against the law.
Innocent children were sent to reform school. Bad guys
turned out good in the end. It was a typical 1930s
melodrama, complete with a dying kid named "Shorty."
But she loved it, and she loved Jack for taking her.

It wasn't long before the relatively unknown Bette
Davis made her appearance as O'Brien's platinum-blonde
love interest. One thing that startled Emma out of her
movie trance was that Davis was so short. Emma
recognized that most all the actresses of this time were
short, and they all had tiny feet. She remembered back to
another time, now in the future, when they visited the

year 1963, and the locals of that time found her feet so unusual. And she was considered tall, even then. Now, four years later, she was probably two inches taller and trying to blend into a time thirty years earlier. There were limits to this time-travel regression, she thought. She would likely be viewed as a circus freak if she went back to the early 10s. Her feet were more telling than her height. Consciously, she uncrossed her legs, dropping her size 11 foot onto the floor and out of Jack's view.

She looked about. Uniformed ushers with electric torches were directing late-arriving patrons to their seats. Many people were feasting on popcorn. No one was smoking. Apparently, this was only allowed in the lobby lounges. Good news for Emma. Her cough was not improving, and she struggled to breathe in any foul air. Just thinking of cigarette smoke caused her to cough again. She had weak lungs, which were being severely tested in 1932's humid, hot, and usually smoky environment. The theater was not air-conditioned and seemed incredibly hot and stuffy to her. But everyone else appeared unaffected, the men wore suits and ties, and the woman dressed well. She knew their bodies were generating heat and sweat beneath all those clothes, but body odor was not an issue for the men and women of the '30s. Her own body was reacting to the crowd, the summer temperatures, and the nearness of Jack. She sensed it giving up liquid life from top to bottom. An unusual sensation for her, but one that was becoming more the norm every day she spent in these times. What the heck, she thought. Like the locals, she had dashed on a bit of cologne before they left...all was well on the olfactory front.

She looked back at the screen and saw Bette Davis looking calm and composed compared with the always frenetic Pat O'Brien. This movie predated the development of Davis' later persona. But her screen presence revealed hints of the aloof affectations that ultimately defined the woman with "Bette Davis Eyes." For now, she was just "arm-candy with a hard edge" for

O'Brien. The movie ended. They left early, skipping the second movie of a double feature. It was just as well for Emma. She was not a big fan of George Raft and needed fresh air. They rode cross-town in Jack's 1930 Buick roadster and dined at a neat restaurant near the National Mall, seated at a quiet little table overlooking the Potomac.

"Lovely, Jack. Lovely."

"Thanks. I'm a regular here. Great view, good food, and a very accommodating wait staff. Glad you're enjoying yourself, Emma. I thought you might be too tired for fun after working with the Sweeny family."

Jack ordered some refreshments before dinner. With a calculated wink to the waiter, he asked for iced tea. The waiter smiled and soon returned with two tall drinks appearing as innocent as a young woman like Emma. She sipped her tea and smiled.

"Say, this is really good, Jack."

"I thought you would like it. It's a fun drink."

Emma whispered across the table, "Any alcohol in here?"

Jack smiled. "Just tea and some special ingredients."

Later Emma found out that this concoction was heavily laced with tequila, vodka, rum, and gin, with heavy alcohol content. She brushed back a lock of her raven hair away from her eye. She was feeling the effects of the "tea." Jack looked very handsome and well-dressed. She had drifted lazily through the meal, talking, smiling, and flirting, relieved to know that her knowledge of "current" events met the test of social conversation. Her repartee with Travers flowed from baseball and movies to women's rights and politics. And she didn't miss a beat, until now. Now, thoughts in her mind were meshing and clouding delightfully.

"Not even a bit, Jack. This is the best medicine for back-breaking work." After dinner, Jack ordered another round of "tea." She took another sip, and he joined her in a toast.

"To the poor and disenfranchised. May they find a

better future..."

Emma smiled. "To a better future..." she said as she bumped her glass into his, somewhat carelessly, emitting a rather loud clank. She giggled and shrugged her shoulders, set down her glass, and reached across the table to hold his hand. "Oh, Jack, you've been so gracious. I'm so pleased we could get together today. And tomorrow, we will meet with Mrs. Roosevelt. I'm so excited. Tell me about her."

Travers leaned forward and moved closer to Emma. His eyes were smiling and responsive. "Must we? I'm much happier talking about you. I know so little. But I feel like I've known you forever."

"Jack Travers..." She smiled and tilted her head. "You do have the gift. You're a born politician. Now come on. Tell me about her. I want to know her before we meet. I want to appear sharp. I've got to explain my idea to her. I've got to know what drives her."

"Don't worry, Emma. You'll get along fine. For one thing, Mrs. R. is another tall glass of lemonade just like you."

Emma was not following him, and her face showed it.

"She's about five-foot-eleven."

"Oh. Really? That's swell."

"You two will fit like two legs in a fine pair of silk stockings. But she's not as smooth as you..." he let his words drift out into the air as if they were some kind of incantation.

Emma ignored his tone. "I like that. Is she politically inclined?"

"That she is. I think she is the perfect match for her husband. He's really a smooth operator. He could charm a snake out of its skin. Eleanor...Mrs. Roosevelt is also charming, but more importantly, she is a dreamer and idealist. She's ahead of her time. She's what I would call a futurist. I think she will help Governor Roosevelt break through the traditional thinking now constricting the world in so many ways. But first, he has to win in November. She is working hard to bring that about."

"Is that why she's in town?"

"That's right. She'll be here tomorrow to speak to the League of Women Voters at lunch. She wants them to get out the vote. She will convince them that the Governor is the man for the 'woman of the future,'" he laughed.

"She sounds like a pip, Jack. I can't wait to meet her tomorrow."

Travers just nodded, requesting the bill and paying for dinner.

They drove along the river. The sun had just set, and the soft, warm evening air flooded the open-top car. She leaned back into the leather seat and stared blankly at the lighted city monuments gracing the colorful horizon. Two days of hard work at Camp Marks helping the Sweeny family had strained her mind and body. But now, all that tension was released. The "tea" and dinner had mellowed her into a state of quiet contentment. This was like a dream, like a Hollywood love story. Jack looked suave in his linen suit, his tan, chiseled features, and how he expertly handled the Buick's floor shift. He moved from gear to gear, smoothly accelerating the car. He was totally in control. She sighed. "What a wonderful evening, Jack."

They walked arm in arm, lazily, beneath the trees. A heavy smell of jasmine filled the air. The darkness and shadows defined the night except for the flickering glow of gas lamps lining the walk. The couple drifted casually along the brick pathway, in and out of the repetitive rings of light. Halfway between, they stopped and kissed in an area of relative darkness. It was not the kind of kiss that a decent man and woman would display to the public. But Emma didn't care, and apparently neither did Jack. Their embrace lasted for a minute, his clothes smelled like him, and body heat fused them together. While his mouth and tongue partnered with hers, his hands gripped her from behind, both high and low. This was all new to Emma and wonderfully exciting. Strangely, she was losing control and enjoying it. Then from nowhere, on the other side of the iron fence lining the walk, a dog rushed up to them, barking loudly and growling. They were startled and then amused. Unable to provoke them, the dog snorted, turned, and trotted away. After laughing aloud, they realized they had broken the silence of the quiet summer evening. They stifled their voices and walked to Jack's house, still arm in arm but tighter, their bodies rubbing each other, their pace quickening with each step.

Once in the confines of Jack's place, he moved quickly but skillfully. Time seemed to slow down for her. She felt terribly lost in the moment. She was flying blind through the fog of romance, and she knew it. It wasn't just the exhaustion from working at the marcher camp or the effects of the drinks, and it wasn't just the sensuous odor of Jack, who stood before her after removing his coat and tie and unbuttoning his shirt. It was like a movie, just like all the great movies she had watched and dreamed about. Reality blended with her imagination and memories of other times and relationships, Garbo and Novarro, Hepburn and Tracy, Bogart and Bergman, Dietrich and Gable—she was hopelessly lost in time and space.

She accepted his offer of a drink. It was hard liquor, something totally new, burning as it went down, igniting a fire of passion inside her. She was incapable and unwilling to resist the movement of their bodies. She was totally aroused. She felt no fear, only excitement and anticipation. Their breathing quickened, and animalistic passions surged. His power over her was intoxicating. His body pressed close, and she felt him possess her, all-consuming and inevitable.

Somehow, he had stripped off his clothes, and she had fallen out of hers with his expert assistance. The pull-down Murphy bed was down, and so were the two lovers. They struggled for positions on the bed. Her lack of experience melted away. He handled everything.

"Jack," her voice revealed her confusion. "Please, Jack. I'm not...."

His long deep kisses quieted her. She felt his body on top of her. Hot, wet skins became one as their breathing and bodies locked into a rhythm. "You are, Emma. You are," he said. And she was.

Slowly, he entered her. She moaned, flinching with the initial pain. She bit her lip, almost enjoying the pain. Then her body relaxed, first accepting, and then welcoming him as she rode a rising cloud of rapture to the top of her world.

Later that night, Jack drove Emma back to her apartment. They didn't have much conversation during the short drive. Jack could handle his liquor well. He showed no negative aftereffects. Emma, on the other hand, was still somewhat dizzy. This was an evening of firsts for her. For one, this was the first time she had ever been drunk. She was flush with nausea and head-spinning disorientation. He walked her to the door. Her movements were unsteady, but he was patient. They stood in silence for a brief moment before he kissed her lightly. "Good night, Emma. I had a wonderful evening." He waited for her to enter the door.

She didn't move. She attempted to gather her senses. "Jack. What about tomorrow? What about Mrs. Roosevelt?"

Jack cleared his throat. "I'm working on that, Emma. But, unfortunately, I am certain Mrs. Roosevelt will not be able to meet with us tomorrow. Maybe Tuesday. I'll talk to you tomorrow. Now get some sleep. I think you need it, my dear." He kissed her again on her forehead.

She struggled to comprehend his words. Finally, she blurted out, "I see...." She turned and looked back quickly. She didn't want him to see the tears in her eyes. "Good night, Jack," she muttered as she opened the door.

-Chapter XII-

Loving Emma

Branko roamed the living room with a cup in hand early that Monday morning. He had found a nearby shop that sold Turkish coffee, and every morning he would prepare a brew of the thick, bitter drink. At these moments, he became a time traveler of sorts. With each sip of the hot mud, he slipped back to his former life in Serbia. As often happened, this feeling was both good and bad for him. But he would take the bad with the good and the sad with the happy. At least he could have emotions now, unlike those times in his life when nothing seemed to matter, when his world was only a black void. Dealing with that nothingness was worse than facing any problem. Now, at least when he dealt with painful issues, he knew he was alive. The black void of the past was a living death.

But the memories always returned. At fifteen, he was recruited into the Serbian Army to fight in the World War. From that moment, every minute of every day, he saw friends and foes killed and maimed. The unending sound of dying horses and men was a chorus from hell. The smoke and odor of burning flesh clung closely and infused his clothing. He could not escape it. Parts and pieces of people spread across the countryside nourished hungry animal and insect scavengers. There were far too many limbs, heads, and bodies for the remaining living to bury. Half the men who served in the Serbian Army and hundreds of thousands of civilians died during the war. Disease, starvation, and the hazards of aimless wandering across their ravaged land killed those who escaped the sabers, bullets, and shells. The people struggled to simply exist. In the end, the hungry animals won the war. At least they had something to eat. Everyone and everything else was lost. For two years, he lived in the black void. Amid the chaos and carnage, dissolving his person was the only way for him to retain his sanity. But ultimately, Branko survived, the war ended, and he regained his humanity. He returned to life, love, and the thick black coffee he enjoyed.

He held the coffee mug in both hands at chest height and gazed out the high window at a mother bird nesting in a tree. He watched her fly away and then return with food for her offspring. The chicks could not be seen, but their loud noises filled the morning solitude. Other sounds drifted in from Emma's room, sobbing, deep, mournful, and muffled cries. He walked to her door and listened, wondering if she was dreaming. But soon, it was clear that she was not. She was crying. He knew she had gone out with Jack Travers last night, and it was late when she returned. He debated and then knocked gently. The sobbing stopped for a moment.

"What?" Emma's voice was faint.

"It is Branko. Are you all right?"

"Yes. Please leave me."

"Can I help?"

"No. I..." she choked on her own words and erupted into a coughing fit. Finally, she spoke again in a tiny voice. "Please. Come in."

He opened the door slowly and entered. Emma sat on the edge of the bed dressed in a nightgown. One look told him that she was in bad shape. Her face was reddened and streaked with tears. Softly, she asked him to close the door. He did and then sat on the bentwood chair facing her.

"Why do you cry?" he asked.

She worked hard to quiet herself. In time, the sniffling stopped, and she could speak clearly.

"I have a problem. But I can't...." She looked up at the ceiling. "I can't talk to the fellows, but I have to talk to someone."

He looked over the top of his coffee cup. "Talk to me. You know. I see you in worst times. And you see worst me. Face to face. We share worlds now, Emma. We share good things. And bad things. Did something bad happen?"

She stammered. "It's not like that. It's more complicated. I'm just a fool."

"You are no fool. You are smart woman. But world is not easy. Every moment are new things to learn. Every moment special. Why are you a fool?"

She dropped her head. "I learned I was not the person I thought I was."

"Who is that?"

She looked confused.

"Who were you?"

"I thought I could always be in control of the situation."

Branko nodded. "But things happened. Like on the train. With the bull..."

"No." she shook her head. "No, not like that at all. Jack is not like that. He's very nice. The fault is in me. I wanted something. I wanted his help, and I thought I could make it work without...."

"Without what?"

"Without. You know."

He thought and then smiled a little. She frowned. He realized she was earnest about this. "Yes, I know. He made you...."

"No...no. That's not it at all. This was not just him. It was us. I really like him, Branko. And I do need his help."

"Does he know what you want?"

"Of course. I just about told him flat out that I expected him to get me an audience with Mrs. Roosevelt. I suppose you could say I even demanded it."

"So he is friend. You asked for great favor. He said yes?"

"Yes."

"But?"

She seemed to think about this question without arriving at an answer.

"But I'm not certain...."

"You think something is wrong?"

"Yes." She sniffled and then blew her nose into a tissue.

"You say 'yes.' And he...?"

"Well. You know..."

He smiled. "I know. Jack is a man. And you are a woman. You like each other. You get romance."

She nodded.

"I understand." He thought for a moment. "You know. I married wonderful woman in Serbia. Before we get married. We make romance. She like and she no like. I...ah...do not understand. I suppose. Now, I am not sure. But I am a man. And men are...well, they are like trees. Big and strong...but full of wood and not so smart." He laughed.

She asked for a sip of his coffee, and he handed her the cup.

She swallowed and grimaced. "How can you drink this?"

"It reminds me of old country." For a moment, she was quiet, and he felt good about himself. She seemed to be settling down and far less upset. She also seemed to be thinking. The real Emma was returning, he thought.

"Branko. Where is your wife?"

He had opened this door. One part of him wanted to slam it shut, but another wanted to talk. He had been in America for three years but had never spoken to anyone about his past. Still, he could not do it. The words would not come out.

"Is she still in Serbia?" asked Emma. No longer was she the coughing, sniffing, hopelessly lost, star struck lover. Her voice was confident but comforting.

"She is," he said. "She is buried there in cemetery. Outside Kruševac."

"Oh. I'm so sorry. I didn't mean to...."

"It is all right, Emma. Many years ago." He shook his head gently.

"Tell me about her."

What could he say about her? She was the most beautiful, talented, wonderful wife, a husband, could ever have. But he didn't know how to express this to the young woman. "She was my wife. My friend. My partner. We work in circus."

"What was her name?"

"Danica."

"She was a trapeze artist?"

"Yes. We flew together." He laughed. "A good life. But hard. We traveled much. But we saw much. We were young. People loved the three of us. They forgot war and all the trouble." His thoughts drifted back five or six years. A clear image of Danica standing on the board wearing the tight red sequined flying suit. Full of life. Proud. Smiling. Beautiful in mind and body. She was accepting the applause of the crowd below. It was thunderous. They were on top of the world.

"The three of you?"

"What?" He didn't even hear her question.

"You said 'the three of you.'"

"Yes." He sipped his coffee. "My brother Dushan. He was part of our act. We were 'The'...how you say it? 'The Flying Brkovic.' I was catcher. They were fliers."

"Oh. So exciting, Branko. You must have really loved her."

"I did, and we all loved circus."

"If you don't mind. How did she die? You don't...."

"No. It is all right." He gathered his thoughts. "Accident. My fault. I was catcher, but I dropped her. She fell fifteen meters and die."

"Oh. I'm so sorry. But it was not your fault. It was a tragic accident...."

"No net."

"What?"

"We work with no net. That was our...how you say... how people knew us. It was my idea. I want us to be famous. In all of Europe, only us fly without net. It was stupid. My fault."

"But..."

"It is OK, Emma. I am OK. But I tell you. Romance like a giant bird. It can grab your head with claws. Then you not think right. I love my wife. But I lost her. I want applause. But Danica die. Everything die. I am fool."

"Branko. I'm sorry I made you think of this."

He pursed his lips. "No mind. I have lost bad thoughts. I only see Danica as beautiful young woman. Like you." He was telling the truth. At least a half-truth. He did see that image of his wife. He always saw it. Every day. But also, not a day would pass without him thinking about his brother Dushan. And about the love affair that Dushan shared with Danica. He couldn't tell Emma what a terrible man he really was. About his incredible vanity and jealousy. About his horrible temper. About his rage and hatred for the both of them. About the dark thoughts that drove him crazy back in the summer of 1927, he accidentally dropped his unfaithful wife to her death. Then the same day beat his brother with bare fists so that Dushan would never be the "pretty boy" again. He could understand the nature of his emotions. He knew about love and romance and the crimes committed in the name of those two tricksters. He was left with an unanswered question. He did not know if her beautiful wrists slipped out of his iron grip or if his strength that terrible day was sapped dry by his intense, evil, and unremitting jealousy? That thought would haunt him for the remainder of his life. He hoped he left that ugly man with the terrible temper behind when he traveled from Serbia to America in 1929. He told himself he would be a new man in a new country. He was, and he was not.

"Branko..."

He came back. "Yes?"

"You are a true friend. I am glad that you have shared with me. I was just a silly girl to even worry about such things. But I am growing up quickly. I get the reality of this world in 1932. Each day, I see better that my problems are mainly in my thoughts. Others have it really bad. You know what I mean?"

Branko nodded. "Young people think they find something new. But we walk same road. We all cross bridges...some sooner...some later. Remember, it is your world, Emma. You run it. You decide. Not men. Not politicians. Not government. Hang on to what you love. Hang on tight. "

"Thank you, Branko."

"Never worry, Emma. I protect you. I help you. No one can hurt you. But Mr. Travers...I think he is your friend. Not enemy. Love is good, Emma. Sometimes exciting. But always good. With no love, we are just big talking bugs."

Emma laughed aloud, and Branko was pleased. She was happy. Then the phone rang. She got up and ran to the living room. Branko followed.

She grabbed the receiver off the hook of the wall phone. "Hello," she said. A pause. "Jack?" Another pause. "She will?" Another pause. "That's fantastic. All right. See you then."

"Good news?" he asked.

Emma smiled. "The best. Mrs. Roosevelt has agreed to meet with us today."

-Chapter XIII-

A Woman's Woman

Branko headed out early that morning to meet with his comrades at Camp Glassford. He asked Zak and Ethan to meet him there at noon. After he left, the time travelers went for a walk. Their basement apartment offered little in the way of comfort. It was cramped, stuffy, hot, and moist. These conditions had been endured by the previous occupants, the servants, but the time travelers found them terribly uncomfortable. Emma still struggled with her cough, and Ethan's nasal passages dripped uncontrollably, gripped by pollen and mold. Only Zak, a man of unique biological construction, was unaffected.

Nothing else was said about Emma's date the previous evening. Zak introduced the subject, implying that she had stayed out late, but Emma brushed off his oblique inquiry. However, there was a discussion about her upcoming meeting with the Governor's wife. And there was some disagreement about the correct approach. Zak pointed out that they only had one chance at influencing Mrs. Roosevelt. Emma would have to gain her favor. Before they left 2032, Ethan had done some historical research on the Roosevelt family with Jacques Dufour. Based on the sketchy information available, he believed that the relationship between the famous New York couple was probably strained. He wasn't sure that they even lived together in 1932. But he was willing to bet that Mr. Roosevelt had had an affair with Mrs. Roosevelt's secretary, a woman named Lucy Mercer.

In 1918, Eleanor Roosevelt discovered some love letters that revealed the extent of the affair. However, pragmatism ruled the day. Divorce discussion was in the air, but Franklin Roosevelt's mother held the money behind the man. She threatened to bankrupt the two of them. Politics was on Mother Roosevelt's mind. The scandal would make her son unelectable. A peace agreement was reached between husband and wife, and life went on. Roosevelt continued his rise to political power, even after being struck down with disabling polio in 1921. And as a result, Eleanor became more involved in the affairs of the country and the world and less concerned about her husband's affairs, which apparently were numerous. The savvy couple worked as partners, if not lovers, until 1932. After that year, which marked the end of his political career, the records of their relationship dried up, and then Franklin Roosevelt died. Mrs. Roosevelt never remarried. Aside from writing occasional magazine articles, she disappeared into the dustbin of history and died sometime in the 1950s.

"From what I have read," said Ethan, "she was an idealist. And her husband was a politician, a smooth-talking glad-hander. She came from money and power. Her uncle was Teddy Roosevelt. A dynamo of a man and a very successful president. I'm guessing she's a straight-shooter. Willing to express her opinions. Sounds like you and Mrs. R have a lot in common."

"I hope so," said Emma. "I'm counting on her."

Mid-afternoon that same day, Jack Travers came by to get Emma. She had done the best she could with her limited wardrobe. This was a big day for her and for history. Jack approved. Although as he looked at her when she opened the door, Emma felt he was looking through her dress as much as at it. Maybe she was too self-conscious. Branko hit it on the head. In 1932, men were men. Not at all like the male population of her time. And she had to admit that, everything considered, Jack's avid interest in her was appreciated on all levels.

For the first time in her life, she felt like a woman. She thought and said things that would never be allowed in the repressive world of 2032. Philosophically, she knew herself very well. But physically and emotionally, she was like a fourteen-year-old experiencing those feelings for the first time. She was a novice woman in training. But she also felt an increasing level of comfort and control. It was almost as if this was the missing link to her person. She was connecting with parts previously unknown. It was an honest self-appreciation. She was a perceptive, intelligent, attractive twenty-one-year-old woman who had traveled back to a time when women, in general, were coming to grips with their place and power in the world. This was an auspicious time, she thought. And she was happy to be a part of it.

"Thanks, Jack," she said nonchalantly.

"How's that?"

"For last night. I had a great time."

He looked over at her, "Not too much drinking?"

"Maybe a little," she said. "But I probably need a little loosening up. I tend to be a bit uptight."

He smiled. "You said it," he said, allowing his words to have many meanings.

Jack was quick-witted, she thought. But I'll play the game. "A gentleman might be slightly more discreet."

Jack pretended to look around. "Who's listening? Anyway, I loved our evening, Emma. Really. You're an exceptional person."

"I hope I'm special to Mrs. Roosevelt."

Jack nodded. "I have a feeling she'll find you most attractive."

Twenty-five minutes later, they pulled up in front of the Mayflower Hotel. He turned the car over to the valet, and soon after, they rode the elevator up to the Presidential suite. Jack knocked gently on the gold-trimmed door. In seconds, the door was opened by a maid who invited them in and announced them to Mrs. Roosevelt. As she walked into the sitting room, Emma was struck by the impressive physical appearance of the forty-seven-year-old woman. Standing about five-foot-eleven, she was a "tall drink," as Jack had labeled her. Her low heels pushed her across the six-foot mark. She would be a very tall woman in any time, thought Emma. While not attractive compared to everyday standards of 1932, she carried herself almost regally. Her hair was full and rich, and her complexion clear and smooth. She had a generous smile that encompassed her broad, fleshy face. It was a Roosevelt smile, wide and welcoming like her uncle and former President, Teddy. Most of all, in Emma's mind, she looked approachable, friendly, and cheerful. Emma liked her from the start.

"You must be Emma," she said. Her voice was cultured and almost sounded affected. But Emma guessed her speech pattern was a product of her heritage. It bespoke of refined power, upper-crust status, and old money.

"I am, Mrs. Roosevelt. Emma Callan-Wright. I am so pleased to meet you." Emma shook her hand gently. Mrs. Roosevelt appeared to be assessing Emma's height. But she said nothing about their commonality.

"And Mr. Travers. As always, it is a pleasure to see you again." Jack shook her hand with deference and formality not seen previously by Emma. Mrs. Roosevelt held his hand as if dancing the minuet and guided him to the center of the parlor. A brief period of social adjustment included directing the maid to serve tea. Emma was in danger of losing her focus in this strange formal social environment. But she sensed Jack was in his element. He appeared at ease and comfortable in the presence of the woman who was the Governor's wife and former President's niece. Small talk graced the conversation while they waited for the tea to be served. Emma noticed a well-built man wearing a black suit moving about in the adjacent room. Apparently a security person, he simply sought a tiny nod from Mrs. Roosevelt. Securing that, he disappeared from view. Tea was served. Emma and Jack were seated across a small table from Mrs. Roosevelt. The sun streamed through the lace curtains behind her. Emma knew that every facial twitch, smile, grimace, or tightening could be read by the older woman, while the bright light behind the hostess would conceal the subtleties of her reactions. Never mind, she thought, just speak honestly and from the heart.

"Thank you again for inviting me," she opened. "And thank you, Jack, for bringing us together today. Let me just state my case briefly. If I may." She looked to Mrs. Roosevelt for permission.

"Please. Proceed," said Eleanor Roosevelt. Her eyes were bright with interest.

Emma swallowed, stifling the urge to cough. She cleared her throat quietly. This was her moment. She quickly glanced at Jack to thank him for making this possible. Then she focused on the wife of Mr. Roosevelt. "I am here because I am very concerned about the veterans who now occupy the city. In my opinion, they have a just cause. But most importantly, they have earned their position. They are simply requesting the early receipt of their World War bonus money. I'm neither a politician nor an expert on the national budget. But I have spent time in their camp. I have seen the discipline that binds these former soldiers together. I have seen their women and children, who have nothing left but their pride and faith in their husbands and fathers. I have seen their dreadful living conditions. And I know they have nowhere to go. This is the end of the line for them. They have personally appealed to the decency of their national leaders. But their appeals have fallen upon deaf ears and empty hearts."

"Go on, my dear."

"Well, I understand there are political ramifications to everything a presidential candidate does. And I believe I understand the position Governor Roosevelt finds himself in concerning the pleas of the veterans. Certainly, the safest position is to avoid taking a stand. No one could accuse Mr. Roosevelt of indifference when in fact the responsibility and response to the veterans is in the hands of the incumbent President and Congress. But..."

"You think the Governor should take a stand because it is the right thing to do. Is that correct?"

"Yes, ma'am. I do." With that, Emma started a cough that could not be stopped. Mrs. Roosevelt poured her a glass of water and offered it to her. Gratefully, she accepted it. She was totally embarrassed by her actions. In time, things stabilized. "I am so sorry. I'm afraid I haven't been able to adapt to the climate here. I am a Northerner. Unaccustomed to the heat and humidity."

"I understand completely," said Mrs. Roosevelt. "I have the same difficulty. Mr. Roosevelt loves the weather in Georgia, but I will never join him there. I could not stand the weather conditions."

Jack Travers spoke. "Emma has spent many days actively helping one of the veteran families, Mrs. Roosevelt. Under those difficult camp conditions, I think the dirt, air, and moisture have had their effect."

"I have no complaints," said Emma. "I'm here because I want to help."

"You know, Emma, a woman is like a tea bag. You never know how strong she is until she gets in hot water. You are strong, Emma. That I can see. And not afraid of hot water." She smiled broadly. "What are you seeking?"

Emma thought for a moment. "I know that the current leaders of our government will do nothing to help the veterans. They have their reasons, which they think are just. But, aside from agreeing with the righteousness of the veterans' cause, I also feel there is an element of danger present in this town. I believe this danger extends far beyond the lives of the veterans, the Communists, the police, or the elected politicians. I think we are on the edge of a precipice. This situation could explode into violence. And violence can lead to unintended consequences."

Mrs. Roosevelt lost her smile. "Jack. I have your most recent report. From that, I did not discern the imminent possibility of violence. At your suggestion, I have been working behind the scenes to get food and medical supplies to the men and their families. What do you think?"

Jack Travers looked at Emma first, then back to his employer. "I think the men are currently under control. I think the Communists would love to foment the situation. Nothing new there. I do agree with Emma. I think it would be best to find a way to get the men to leave Washington.

No good will come from their continuing presence. Their bonus is dead. But they cannot accept that. And Mr. Hoover appears to be more than concerned. He may be frightened. Apparently, there are orders from the local officials for the protesters to evacuate. But at the moment, it is a cat and mouse game. No one knows how to get movement without creating consequences. My understanding is that Commander Waters needs more time to demobilize, but the government is reluctant to grant it."

"Mrs. Roosevelt. If your husband could only promise that if elected, he would find a way to pay the bonus, no one would lose face. The marchers would have a reason to leave, and the local officials would see the light at the end of the tunnel. Even President Hoover might be forced to jump on the bandwagon to match Governor Roosevelt's proposal and ratify the possibility of payment rather than be left in the dust. I know this suggestion opens Mr. Roosevelt to cries of grandstanding. But what would you prefer? A little political ammunition for the opposition, or martial law and the cancellation of the election?"

"What do you mean, Emma?" asked Mrs. Roosevelt. This comment seemed to puzzle her. She cast her eyes on Jack.

"I mean…"

Travers jumped in. His face was flushed. "Emma, please do not exaggerate the situation. We must maintain a reasonable approach. You're creating a fantasy world. We didn't invite you here to…."

"No. No, I am not, Jack. We live in a world that is filled with fear. Filled with men who want power. Look at Italy. Look at Germany. It could happen here. Americans are disenfranchised people. People who are begging for solutions. Politicians like President Hoover never lower themselves to serve the common man, but the common man is just waiting for an excuse to do something…anything. All across the nation, people are waiting. Waiting for someone to do something." Emma looked at Mrs. Roosevelt, who seemed entranced by the debate. "I'm sorry, Mrs. Roosevelt. But you must understand. The future of this country and the political future of Franklin Delano Roosevelt may be determined in this room today."

"Don't apologize, Emma. The future belongs to those who believe in the beauty of their dreams and the ugliness of their nightmares. I see what you are saying. I appreciate your conviction and concern for the people who have little of anything and no real representation. I don't think I am going out on a limb to say that my husband recognizes there are forces in this great land of ours who wouldn't mind some centralized command. There are powerful people who might jump at the chance to simplify the government. In their minds, unhappy, jobless, homeless people are dangerous. You are correct. These veterans are a symbol of hope and despair. And that has been the nexus of revolution throughout history." She looked at Travers. "Jack, I'm most impressed with your friend Emma. Maybe she is reaching in her conclusions, but they come from her heart. They also have logic behind them. I will discuss this matter with Mr. Roosevelt when I return to New York tomorrow. Emma, you are a woman of principle and determination. Something I admire very much."

At that moment, there was a rather loud knock. The maid opened the door, and another tall woman with a commanding presence entered. She had dark, close-cropped hair and was big-boned with a schoolmarm look. Jack Travers leaped up when he saw her enter.

"Hick. What are you doing here?" asked Mrs. Roosevelt.

"Sorry for barging in, but I was invited here by Mr. Travers. Right, Jack? I'm just running a little behind schedule." She walked up to the trio who were all standing now. The woman reached out to Mrs. Roosevelt, and they shook hands. Jack did the same. And then the woman laid her eyes upon Emma. "Oh. Mrs. Roosevelt. I see you have a new guest. And a pretty one, she is."

"Yes. Yes. Emma Callan-Wright, this is Lorena Hickok.

She is a reporter for the Associated Press covering the election and a good friend of mine."

"Pleased to meet you, Mrs. Hickok," said Emma as she extended her hand to shake. The woman's handshake was firm, almost manly.

"My friends call me 'Hick.' You can call me Lorena...that is, until we become friends."

"Let's all sit down," said Mrs. Roosevelt, expressing some distress. "We were just discussing the situation of the Bonus Marchers with Emma. She has the idea that I should ask Franklin to help them, or at least promise to help." They sat.

Lorena Hickok asked the maid for a drink. "My usual," she said. While waiting, she lit a cigarette and abruptly posed a question to Emma. "Why would Franklin D. Roosevelt want to expose himself to ridicule and accusations when this whole thing plays out in his favor just the way it is?" Her drink arrived. Apparently, nobody in Washington cared about the prohibition laws, thought Emma. The woman, "Hick," as Mrs. Roosevelt called her, downed half of the whisky in one gulp. "So...what's the answer, Emma?"

Emma wanted to answer but sensed she should hold her tongue.

Eleanor Roosevelt looked flustered.

"Lorena, may I see you for a moment...in private." It wasn't a question.

"Sure...Mrs. Roosevelt. Let's adjourn." She blew a puff of smoke in Emma's direction.

The two women removed themselves from the room, leaving Jack and Emma to stare at each other. Emma whispered to Jack, "Who is that?"

Jack smiled. "She is a new but dear friend of the Governor's wife."

"Why did you invite her here? At this moment." Emma started coughing again. In time, she quelled the demands of her body's automatic response to the cigarette smoke.

"Are you all right?" he asked.

She drank some water and responded. "Why?" she

asked again.

"Listen, Emma," he spoke quietly. "You don't invite that woman. She just invites herself. I mentioned the meeting, and well, here she is."

They sat in silence for several minutes before the two women returned. Emma and Jack stood.

"I'm afraid I must bid you both goodbye. Mrs. Hickok, quite properly, has reminded me that we are running late for our train back to New York." She looked at Emma and extended her hand. "It was a pleasure to meet you, Emma, and I will give your ideas serious consideration. I hope you enjoy your stay here in Washington."

Emma looked at the lady reporter. She was smiling out of the corners of her mouth. Realizing that the meeting was over, Jack was in ushering mode. He guided Emma toward the door.

"Please do consider this, Mrs. Roosevelt. It's essential for everyone's future," said Emma on the way out.

"I will, Emma. I will."

Emma listened to her words. However, they had lost the ring of truth that had characterized their conversation before that woman had arrived. Mrs. Roosevelt had changed. In just a few moments, her energy, independence, and bravado had dimmed with the appearance of the Hickok woman. She wondered what that was all about.

Jack drove back to Emma's apartment and parked in front. They hadn't said much during the ride home. Emma was still puzzled by her encounter with American royalty. "Did I do something wrong today?"

"With Mrs. Roosevelt?"

"Yes."

"No."

"Then why did everything seem to evaporate in front of my eyes? Things were going so well. I really enjoyed her. And she seemed to like me also."

Jack smiled. "That's the rub, Emma. She did enjoy you. It was obvious."

"What's with Mrs. Hickok? When she showed up, our whole conversation seemed to grind to a halt. Did I say something?"

Jack tugged at the collar of his shirt. "How can I put this?" He raised his eyebrows. "Let's just say that Mrs. Roosevelt's relationship with Mrs. Hickok is special."

Emma was puzzled. "You mean 'special' like that?" Her eyebrows arched.

Jack nodded. "I think so...."

"So that woman is jealous of me? That's what this is all about? The lives of millions of people hang in the balance because the Governor's wife might find me attractive?"

"Emma, this is Washington, D.C." He shrugged. "It's the epicenter of American politics. But politicians, their wives, and their girlfriends are all people. And people are people. They're real flesh and blood. That's the reality of things. Maybe you're just a wee bit idealistic."

Emma stared ahead blankly. "I'm just honest, Jack. I'm just concerned about the future of this country. I would hope that you would be too."

"Hey, don't jump on me. Other women wouldn't be so catty if you weren't such a sweet kitten. And I am very concerned about the future of America. Anyway, no one is without sin when it comes to this town. Even you."

She spun her head around and faced him. "What do you mean by that, Mr. Travers?"

He looked like a cat with a canary in his mouth. "I mean. Everyone in Washington has their secrets, dear. Even you...right?"

Emma sensed trouble. She wondered where Jack was going with this. Had she made a mistake? Maybe it was something simple, a slip of the tongue, one errant word about the future. Or maybe it was something Ethan had said. Or perhaps even Zak. She somehow suspected that Jack could understand at least some of the sign language. And Zak and her brother were very cavalier when using their hands to talk. She coughed just to buy time to think. Then she coughed for real.

"You OK?" he asked.

She swallowed. "I'm OK," she said, but she was not. She was very concerned. "What secrets?" she asked, almost afraid to get a response.

"I thought so," he said. "I knew something was going on. I can see it in your face. Your story has a few holes in it."

"What story?" asked Emma. "What are you talking about?"

"You forget," he said with a smile, "I've seen your undergarments."

"Jack. Now you've lost me."

He smiled. "Call me a detective, but from the moment I first met you, I knew that you couldn't be what you pretended to be."

"Yes. And what was I pretending to be?"

"You know. A penniless, out-of-work rail-rider," he answered.

She listened and relaxed.

"And, when I looked at the tags on your new lingerie, I could tell that you were accustomed to the finer things in life and that you had the funds to afford them. Ah...*Pareee*."

"Jack Travers. I can't believe you. Reading the tags on my underwear."

"Don't worry, Emma. I won't tell my landlord. The apartment is yours. But don't forget me."

"Oh, I won't forget you. You..." She said with mock anger. "You and your detective work. Any excuse to wiggle me out of my underwear. So you can check my labels." She shook her head.

He smiled and nodded knowingly. "You bet. I'm a regular Hercule Poirot. It's nice work for the detective, too."

"So you figured out that we brought some money from home."

"No, I get it. You're dedicated to the marcher cause. You wanted to blend in. To be accepted. And I guess it's a good idea to look impoverished if you're going to ride the rails and live in poverty. For one thing, you don't want to get robbed."

"All right. You found out our secret. But don't tell Branko. He would drop us like a hot potato if he found out we tricked him."

"My lips are sealed," he said. "I'll only unseal them for you...on special occasions."

She leaned over and kissed him on the lips. "Merry Christmas, Hercule." She kissed him again. "And Happy New Year too."

-Chapter XIV-

A Man's Man

Late in the afternoon on July 26th, Branko, in the company of Ethan and Zak, had just ended another meeting with the downtown Communist activists. Among other things, the Communists had discussed their potential role in the impending evacuation. As always, the juxtaposition of opposing forces, the police, and the protesters could be an opportunity for the Communists to grab power, but only if they could gain the veterans' confidence. Ultimately, it was decided that they would have to play the waiting game. They were small in number, and their success depended on timing and luck. Everyone was directed to stand ready.

The time travelers and Branko were headed home from the meeting when they were grabbed. Three men in a black sedan presented their badges, ordered them into the car, and drove them to the Justice Department building. Separated from Branko, Ethan and Zak were placed in a holding room at the United States Bureau of Investigation headquarters. Initially, two agents questioned them for a few minutes. Nothing too scary, all very business-like, simple questions, straightforward answers. Then the agents left the room, and the two young men sat unguarded and unattended for about an hour. The western sun poured through the closed windows of the room that had no air conditioning, and it became a furnace. Finally, it was too much for Ethan. He opened the office door, seeking assistance.

In seconds, he was approached by a man who demanded to know where he was going.

"Hey, it's like an oven in here. And we need to use the washroom."

"Not used to the heat, eh? Come with me," he said.

The burly agent escorted them to the washroom and sent them in, one at a time. Afterward, he brought them back to the same office. The original interviewing agents had returned. Even in the oppressive heat, they continued to wear their dark blue suit coats over their white shirts and ties, all neat and tidy.

"Thank you, Agent Thomson..." said Carr.

The big guy left the room, but he remained stationed outside, his shadow visible in the frosted glass upper panel of the door.

"So, you boys have been socializing with the socialists? Eh?"

Ethan responded. "We have visited with them. We told you that. Is that against the law?"

"All depends," said Carr, who sat across from them.

During this conversation, the other agent walked behind Zak and Ethan and, without warning, reached down and grabbed Zak's butt with both hands. Abruptly, the young mute leaped out of his chair. Astonished and surprised, he swung around, seeking his attacker. But he uttered no sound.

Startled, Ethan looked at Zak, wondering what had happened.

Zak signed furiously. *"This guy just goosed me! What the hell is going on?"*

"I guess you're getting special *personal* treatment from the Bureau, Zak." Ethan looked back to Carr. "Is this standard procedure?"

The agent ignored his question. "What do you think, Westbrook? Is he faking?"

"No, he's legit. Not a peep," said Westbrook. "Sit down, Mr. Newman. You passed the test."

Zak shook his head and made a face while Westbrook physically guided him back into his chair.

"Zak can't talk. I told you that. No voice box. OK?" said Ethan.

"All right. Fine. We'll talk to you, Mr. Wright. Or is it ..." Carr looked at his notes. "Mr. Callan-Wright?"

"That's right. Callan-Wright."

Zak signed something.

"What did he say?" demanded Westbrook.

"He said 'right.'" Ethan chuckled.

"Very funny. It won't be so funny when we book you," said Carr.

"We haven't done anything," said Ethan. "And where is our friend Branko?"

Agent Carr stood up again. Both agents towered over the seated time travelers with an air of intimidation. Then, Carr leaned in, bringing his face uncomfortably close to Ethan's as he spoke softly. "Mr. Brkovic...he's a special case. But, of course, you must know that."

"Know what? We don't know much about him. Except that he saved my sister's life when we rode the rails to get to Washington. We're just here to help the veterans."

"So you don't know anything about Mr. Brkovic?"

"Hey. We didn't even know his name until now. He's just Branko to us."

"And he never showed you his card?" asked Westbrook.

"Card?"

"Communist Party member. Joined in 1921."

Ethan looked at Zak, who raised his eyebrows. "Nope. Didn't know about that. But what of it? Is that against the law?"

"I'll be asking the questions, Mr. Wright," said Carr. He returned to his chair. "You seem to be bright boys. Even though Mr. Newman can't talk, he seems to get the picture. Carr pulled out a pack of cigarettes and offered them to the time travelers. Both Ethan and Zak declined. He put the pack back into his pocket. "So you two are in town to help the veterans. Obviously, you are not veterans. At least not World War veterans. So what's your game? Educated college boys who espouse the Communist doctrine? Something wrong with America? Are you looking to overthrow the government of the United States? You here to cause trouble?"

Zak was disturbed by the tone of the agent's questions. He also knew that the time travelers' credentials would not stand up to any real investigation, especially that of Hoover's men. His wallet included a library card, an expired college identification card, an aged Boy Scout membership card, a phony folded-up job rejection letter, a few crumpled dollars, and a couple of purposely beat-up, staged, sepia-tone family photos. Luckily it also contained a freshly printed business card from Jack Travers. That little piece of information was solid, authentic, and contemporary and would be simple to verify. Ethan had similar minimal documents.

Their story was that they had been college students from Portsmouth at the University of New Hampshire, but they gave up the quest for education when jobs and money became scarce. Now they were part of the great unwashed jobless wanderers. This alleged status was obviously not unusual for the times. Zak was not concerned about being labeled Communists or agitators but worried about their fabricated personal histories. If these were deeply explored by the Feds, they would raise unanswerable questions. If they were held for an extended time, even a week or two, it could jeopardize their return to the future. As far as they knew, the *TimeTravelle* worked for twenty-eight days of time travel; no more and half of their allotted time had already passed. They had no desire to test the limits of the 1932 legal system. If their detainment turned into anything more complicated, involving lawyers, background checks, or anything else, they would be in big trouble.

"Zak and I are loyal Americans," said Ethan. "We're not Communists. We came to Washington because we had nothing else to do. We can't get jobs. We were intrigued by the Bonus Marcher movement, so we came here. This fellow Branko is somebody we met catching a freight train. He did help out my sister, but other than that, we don't know much about him. Our only crime was to follow him around."

Ethan had tossed Branko under the bus, but Zak knew he had no choice.

"There's food in Camp Glassford. Those Communists

have food, and we get hungry. We didn't study political science in school. To be honest, we don't care about politics."

"What about this Branko fellow? What does he have to do with the Communists? What do you know about their plans?"

"Nothing. Really. Those people think we're friends of Branko, but they don't tell us anything. As a matter of fact, the head guy, Mr. Pace, told us that Branko will give us directions."

"And?" asked Westbrook.

"And. Nothing. We just wander around, grabbing some grub when we can. We listen to the speeches to be polite. I don't know. They know we've attended college. Maybe that looks good to them. Most of the guys hanging around there don't have much education. I get the feeling that they're looking for anyone to fill their ranks. But the fact is that we're just moochers."

Agent Carr nudged his partner, and they left the room. Zak and Ethan were alone.

"Sorry, Zak. But we can't be sucked into this whole Communist thing. We didn't do anything. This guy Branko is a hot potato. I don't want any part of it." His voice was loud enough to be heard by anyone monitoring the door. Zak winked to acknowledge that he understood Ethan's approach. After a few minutes, the door opened again. This time the two agents were joined by a third man who dressed elegantly, wore a scowl, and was obviously in charge. Of medium height, he wore a dark blue tailored suit, a vest, a finely crafted shirt, a double-pointed vest-pocket handkerchief, and a crisply knotted tie. Ethan spotted a gold Masonic pin on his lapel. He had perfectly coiffed hair. When he stared at Ethan, the look on his face was intense, but it softened when he glanced at Zak.

"Gentlemen, this is the Director, Mr. Hoover."

J. Edgar Hoover talked fast and got to the point. "You two have been brought here because you have been associating with known agents of the Communist Party.

It is quite clear that these people have come to Washington to cause trouble. And you could be in intense trouble unless you cooperate fully with us. Do you understand?"

"Definitely, Mr. Hoover. We understand."

"We're going to call your parents. Maybe they can help you balance your priorities."

Ethan and Zak both reacted. And the three men appeared to sense their instant discomfort.

"I can see that you don't like that idea," said Hoover. He now wore a strange smile as if he had discovered a weakness to be exploited.

"Look. Please, Mr. Hoover. We don't want our parents involved. They have it tough enough as it is without worrying about us. Couldn't you just check with Mr. Travers? He works for Governor Roosevelt. He found us a place to live. He'll vouch for us."

Hoover looked at the time travelers like they were two mutts in a dog show, and he was the judge. "Agent Carr, get ahold of this Travers. We've spent enough time on these two. Give Mr. Callan-Wright a cup of coffee and a magazine. I want to see Mr. Newman in my office."

"Sir. He can't talk. He's a mute," said Carr.

"I know that, Agent Carr. Thank you. Just escort him to my office in fifteen minutes."

"Yes, sir."

Hoover turned to look back. His eyes drifted toward the ceiling. "Was an agent smoking in this room?" he asked.

Carr quickly responded. "No, sir."

Hoover just nodded. He walked out in small, measured, almost robotic steps, like an officious penguin, thought Zak.

Precisely fifteen minutes later, Zak and Agent Carr entered the anteroom of the Office of the Director of the Bureau of Investigation. A secretary guarding the door announced their presence into a desktop intercom box. A man's voice squawked back from the unit's speaker.

"You may enter, gentlemen," she said.

They entered the inner sanctum, a quiet corner office, and found J. Edgar Hoover sitting regally in a high-backed black leather chair like a potentate. His oversized desk maintained a proper distance between him and any visitor. The lighting was subdued and concealed. The walls were paneled with highly polished dark oak, and impressive and overstuffed furniture sat on the dark blue and white terrazzo floor. Thick navy blue drapes darkened the space. It had the feel of a mortuary viewing room. Agent Carr stood next to Zak, obediently awaiting orders from his boss.

"That will be all for the moment, Agent Carr."

Carr slipped away like a minion, silently retreating out of the office.

"Sit down, please, Mr. Newman."

Zak sat in one of the two chairs in front of the desk. As his frame sunk into the upholstery, he realized that Hoover's chair was elevated while his chair was low. He felt like a kid in the principal's office.

Hoover closed the open manila folder atop his desk and placed it in the credenza behind him. He sat erect and rigid. Zak noticed the entirely unnecessary cast-bronze nameplate that graced the top of the desk: *J. Edgar Hoover, Director*. There was nothing else on the desk except for the intercom box.

"So, Mr. Newman. I understand you can't talk. But I can tell by the look in your eyes that you are a bright boy." Hoover's coal-black eyes looked deeply into Zak's. He held his gaze for many seconds as if contemplating something before speaking again. "So I'll do the talking, and you do the listening."

Zak nodded and smiled.

"You're not a smoker, are you?"

Zak shook his head.

"Good. Good. I don't like smoking. You have a bright smile. I like that in a young man. And you seem to be at ease within this environment. Unusual...but welcome. Most men who sit opposite me are unsteady, wavering, and fearful. But I don't detect that in you. You have a calmness about you that might confirm your innocence. Are you innocent, Mr. Newman?"

Zak knew the answer. He nodded.

"I thought so. I didn't think you and your friend would be involved with these Communist agitators. You know our job is to stop the march of the international Communist menace. I can assure you it is real and pervasive. It is a threat to every God-fearing man, woman, and child in this country. The destruction of our American form of government. The destruction of American democracy. The destruction of free enterprise. And it stands for the creation of a "Soviet Union United States" and worldwide revolution. Do you understand this, young man?"

Zak maintained a pose of rapt attention and nodded.

"Very good. Publicly, these Communists say they do not advocate force and violence. They say that when they are only defending themselves, they're accused of using force and violence. This is a lot of double-talk. They're here now for one reason, and one reason alone, to cause trouble. I don't blame the veterans for coming here, but I do blame their naiveté. They have allowed the Communists to infiltrate their organization. They have been duped. Unwittingly, young people like you are often used as tools. The Communists know you are the future of their grand plan. If they convince you that there is something wrong with our system of government because you cannot get employment and you are experiencing difficult times, then they will have your mind. You must resist. Will you resist, Zak? You don't mind me calling you by your first name, do you?" Again, he studied Zak's reaction to his diatribe.

Zak smiled. He gave a quick head shake to indicate he was not concerned about Hoover's informality. The only thing Zak was thinking at this moment was that J. Edgar Hoover was a very insecure man.

"Good. That's good, Zak." He paused. "I'm not boring you with this statement of my mission, am I?"

Zak shrugged his shoulders, smiled lightly, and shook

his head. He knew the drill. He understood this man completely. It came with the territory. He knew he was young, especially good-looking, and apparently innocent and defenseless. It was an attractive combination to certain people. The one-sidedness of the conversation was not a problem. For a narcissist such as J. Edgar Hoover, Zak was the perfect listener. For another ten minutes, Hoover continued droning on about the vital role he played in the country's defense and his battle against the Communists.

Then he stopped cold. "You must never have any additional contact with this Serbian Communist, Mr. Brkovic. Do you understand?"

Zak knew the correct head movement.

"Are you staying near here?"

Zak was about to nod when a woman's voice came over the intercom. "*Mr. Tolson is here, sir.*"

Hoover's face looked pained. "Send him in."

A man entered who was another dandy-type, only taller and much better looking. He looked at Zak. "Oh. I didn't mean to interrupt, sir." He kept his eyes on Zak. He walked up to the desk. He stood close to Zak, who found he was staring directly at Tolson's butt. He felt the heat emanating from the man's body. Tolson looked down on him, stressing his overbearing physical position.

"Not a problem, Mr. Tolson. I was just informing young Mr. Newman about the dangers of Communism."

"Yes...I see..." said Tolson. "Well, in my role as Assistant Director, I have personally met with Mr. Travers and Miss Callan-Wright, the sister. I believe we can be sure that these young men will not be contacting the Communist contingent within the protestors again, sir. Mr. Travers, who is employed by Governor Roosevelt, has assured us of his complete cooperation. He will assume responsibility for their future activities."

"Very well, Mr. Tolson. And the Communist?"

"He has been provided more permanent accommodations. I will personally handle that matter, sir." Tolson looked at Zak. "Well, young man, you are free to go." He glanced back at Hoover. "That is, sir, if you have completed your discussions with the young man."

Looking more like a bulldog than before, Hoover scrunched up his face and answered with some resignation, "Yes, Mr. Tolson." He looked at Zak. "You may go now, son. But remember what I told you."

Zak nodded and thought, what was that all about? But he knew. His special ultra-human sensors were high, dry, and operating at peak efficiency. He shook Hoover's tiny hand and exited. Tolson stayed and carefully watched him leave. The door closed behind Zak, and he could only speculate about the conversation the two men might be having. But he suspected the topic was not Communism.

-Chapter XV-

Ready to Rumble

The reunion between brother, sister, good friend Zak, and Jack Travers was emotional. Ethan hugged Emma. Emma hugged Zak. And Travers watched over them like a mother hen. From his perspective, the lobby of the Justice Department building was an inappropriate venue for public demonstrations of relief and happiness. He eased them toward the exit. Because the building was now closed, the guard at the door required that they sign out. After hastily scribbling their names, Zak and Ethan flew through the revolving door and hit the fresh air and freedom. Ethan called out a war-whoop. Travers shook his head. What would these guys ever do if they faced real jail time?

Outside, they all walked away from J. Edgar Hoover's headquarters, crossing the long shadows cast by the Justice Department building. Ahead, Ethan and Zak horsed around like two kids, while Emma and Travers followed. Cruising in the sky above, a single-engine Potomac Flying Service monoplane glistened, its silvery skin caught in the rays of the late evening setting sun. The sound of its motor bounced off the walls of the building behind, magnifying the effect of its airborne majesty.

"Look," said Travers to Emma. He pointed to the way of the future in the sky above. "For three bucks a person, we could fly over D.C. Would you do it?"

"In a heartbeat, Jack, but I'm already flying high."

They walked arm in arm. She pulled him close, and they stumbled and double-stepped like two drunks. They laughed. In front of them, Ethan and Zak were still gawking at the airplane. The four crossed the street, and Jack directed them to his car, parked in a government lot.

His Buick roadster gleamed.

"Great tin can, Jack," Ethan almost shouted in excitement.

Jack opened the passenger-side door. Emma, her movements slow, slid into place. He closed the door and looked at her. She didn't look well. Maybe it was just the strain of the day's events or the result of her work in the marcher camp. Whatever it was, he would get her to bed early tonight. He turned around and found Ethan and Zak. They looked lost.

"Where are we going to sit?" asked Ethan. "No ride for us?"

"No problem. Just hop in the rumble seat," said Jack. The two young men looked befuddled. "In the back. It's open. Go ahead."

Ethan and Zak stared at the rear of the Buick, waiting for it to reveal its secrets. Obviously, they needed help. Travers quickly walked behind the car, grabbed the handle on the back deck, and flipped open the panel to reveal the concealed seat. "What's the matter, boys? They don't have rumble seats where you come from?"

"Sorry, Jack. I think we're still in a daze from our interrogation," said Ethan. "You know, Zak even had the big guy, J. Edgar Hoover, all over him."

"I'll bet," said Travers.

Zak hopped onto the foot pad above the back bumper and made his way into the elevated seat. Ethan followed his lead. As Travers rounded the back of the car, he looked at the two friends sitting in the rumble seat like two frogs on a rock. He wondered what kind of young men did not understand the everyday workings of his car. These two had a lot to learn. It was a good thing he came to their aid today, or they would be spending the night in jail. He jumped into the driver's seat and glanced at Emma. "How are you feeling? You look a bit pale." He put his hand on her forehead. "A bit warm, too."

She smiled weakly and answered in a quiet voice. "Sorry, this has been a rough day. I'll be fine. I'm just a little tired. And Jack..."

"Yes."

"Thank you for saving the day." She leaned her head back and sighed with relief and appreciation.

"You're most welcome. I hope we can keep the Hardy Boys out of trouble."

Emma rolled her eyes. "Me too. They are a handful."

Jack swung his arm over the seatback to get a better view. "Time for a little come to Jesus meeting."

Ethan jumped on Travers' line of thinking, cutting him short. "Jack, we're not particularly religious, if you know what I mean."

"It's a figure of speech, Ethan. Really, sometimes I'd swear you were born on another planet. Stay with me now. OK?"

Ethan nodded. Jack realized he would have to spell things out. "So, a couple of big things happened today," he said. "One, Emma was able to meet with Mrs. Roosevelt and pass on her thoughts about helping the marchers. I can't be sure Mrs. Roosevelt will discuss this matter with the Governor. Or if she does pass on Emma's proposal, whether he would have any interest. I know you all have your heart in the right place. But it's a cruel world out there."

"We know about that, Jack. That's why we're here," said Ethan. "We want to make a difference."

Travers nodded and continued. "Politics is a messy business, and politicians often benefit more from the mistakes of their rivals than from the brilliance of their own deeds. Governor Roosevelt is a master politician. He knows President Hoover is drowning in his inflexibility about the Bonus Marchers. The voting public is definitely sympathizing with their cause. This encampment is symbolic of all the Hoovervilles. In movie theaters across the country, newsreel cameras have captured the spirit of the veterans. The man on the street is not concerned with the national budget. He can't comprehend that. But he understands shanty living, abject poverty, and stuffy politicians. And parents unable to feed their babies. He knows what it is like to be kicked out of his home. All of this is President Hoover's mess. And I am almost certain that Governor Roosevelt will choose not to interject himself into any of it. Hoover is like an elephant stuck in quicksand. In the eyes of the public, the more he battles, the faster he sinks."

"Why would he let that happen?" asked Emma.

"So long as he is in control and has his strength, there is the possibility that the elephant will find firm ground and walk out of the mud. If not, then history will decide his fate. But remember, there is history...and there is the interpretation of history. Whatever happens, Mr. Hoover will do his best to mold the message of history in his favor. He is the president of the United States, and most Americans want to see the world through his eyes. Not through the eyes of Lowell Thomas or *Movietone News*."

"But what about the danger that this could all blow up, Jack? Why not stop it now by giving these men hope and self-respect?" Emma said weakly.

Jack looked into Emma's eyes lovingly. "You are a wonderful person, Emma. And that may well be a fine idea for Mr. Hoover to implement, but that is his decision. He's a smart politician, too, and there is no way he will push this mass of men too far. It's a dance. It's what these men do. They are very good at it. In the end, the marchers will go. Maybe not without some struggle. But they will leave. This will end. But it will always have a stink associated with it, and that smell will stay with President Hoover. If he was just a little smarter...."

"But if he was smart, he would be offering a way out," responded Emma. "He would be meeting with the marchers. He would at least be that smart."

"Well," said Jack. "What can I say?' He smiled. "Sometimes...I should say 'always' with politicians, the ego is bigger than the man."

Ethan leaned forward and erupted. "What about the Communists? They could pop things open, in a bad way, any moment."

"Please, Ethan. I promised that you and Zak would stay away from the Communists. I put my word on the line and Mr. Roosevelt's reputation. You understand that, don't you? I'm responsible for you now. Please don't do anything rash. The Communists are closely watched by every cop and federal officer in Washington. There are only a few hundred of them. If they cause any trouble, and I mean *any* trouble, they're on their own. The veterans will not stand with them. They will be scooped up like fish in a barrel and eaten for dinner. Trust me, Mr. J. Edgar Hoover and his men are just waiting for the opportunity to make headlines."

Ethan leaned back in the rumble seat and made a face. But Travers knew he got it. Jack looked back at the two young men sitting tall in the saddle. "You fellows ready?"

Zak and Ethan straightened up. "You shred it, wheat," said Ethan.

They motored out of the lot and headed for the apartment. It had been a long day. As he drove along the streets of Washington, Jack Travers felt he had things under control. His new young friends were finally adapting to his line of thinking, and it looked like they would stay out of trouble. He gained energy from the dynamic current events surrounding his life. He was a man of action and in the midst of it. The Roosevelts, the Hoovers, the protesters, and the Communists were all part of the great game of life. And Emma was a wonderful part of the game. He was in the right spot at the right time, and he knew it.

But tonight, he looked forward to a quiet evening at home, drinking some decent Scotch whisky and listening to the *Lux Radio Theater*. Work was over for the day. By now, Mrs. Roosevelt was on a train heading north, rumbling through the night to New York. He could imagine her and her friend Hick passing the time playing cards in the club car, sipping a little contraband whisky, giggling at each other's humor, and shooting conversational double entendres back and forth like tiny cupid's arrows. At this moment, they were too busy to need the opinions of Jack Travers. He glanced over to Emma and thought about his own romance. He felt close to the pretty young woman who had fallen into his life. And he was worried about her. He knew this urge was moving him into the arena of conflict between the requirements of his job and Emma's needs and desires. He knew her desires were beginning to match his. He had not expected this to happen. She was not the first woman in his life. There had been many, but he had never felt these feelings before. He gripped the wheel and shook these thoughts out of his head. As he shifted gears, he remembered Branko. The Serbian wasn't as lucky or innocent as the Twins and Zak. No one could vouch for him; he was alone and remained a prisoner of the other Hoover.

The small man with the large black mustache stepped forward when the guard called his name: "Gvozden Brkovic."

"I am Brkovic," he said. He held his head low with disdain for the process.

The dog-faced guard positioned him in front of the counter with the ink pad and forms. "Relax. This is standard Bureau procedure. Any of our guests who stay the night get the treatment. Left hand first...."

Branko went through the fingerprinting drill. He was now part of the national identification system. As he wiped his hands clean with a solvent-soaked rag, he knew he was being drawn into the world of the police and their ways. They were the same everywhere. They spoke the same language and shared the same low opinion of the average man. In their minds, everyone had something to hide, and every man needed to be watched and controlled.

Agent Carr grabbed him by the elbow and directed him to an interrogation room. Once in the tiny windowless space, Carr pointed to a chair before a stark wooden table. Branko sat. A single bare bulb light fixture hung above. There was nothing else in the room except for two other chairs. The agent sat across from him. They looked at each other.

"Just a minute, my friend, and we'll get started," said

Carr.

They sat in silence for a few minutes. Branko listened to the sound of his rapid breathing. His heart pounded; he could smell the sweat of fear soaking his armpits. He anticipated the worst. He had experienced interrogations in Serbia, and they had not been pleasant.

Finally, the door swung open, and Clyde Tolson entered the room. He did not shake hands with the prisoner. He didn't even acknowledge his presence. "Agent Carr. He has been processed?"

"Yes, sir."

"Very good." The tall man stood at the end of the table. He looked at Branko. "I am Special Agent Tolson. I am the Assistant Director of the United States Bureau of Investigation."

Branko nodded.

"I'll bring you up to date quickly, Mr. Brkovic." Tolson sat in the remaining chair directly across from Branko. "You are now in our custody. That means you are in the custody of the United States government. Do you understand?"

Branko nodded.

"Speak, please."

"Yes, I do."

"Good. You are a citizen of Serbia. Is that correct?"

"Yes, I have filled out papers...."

"Yes, yes. You would like to become a citizen."

"I would." The heat was building in the confined space. Branko felt perspiration beading on his forehead. He wiped his brow with a handkerchief.

"Well. What you say tonight, in this room, may determine that possibility," said Tolson, his voice flat and emotionless. "May I have the document?" Carr retrieved the evidence from a manila envelope. Delicately, Tolson snatched the small, aged wallet card out of Carr's fingertips and inspected it with great interest, first the front, then the back. He held it between his thumb and forefinger and waved it in front of Branko. "Now, I'm no expert in the nuances of your native tongue, Mr. Brkovic, but this appears to be an authentic membership card in the Communist Party of Serbia. Is that true?"

"I was. It is. Yes, I was member. But this is old card. I was young man. Many years ago."

"So you declared yourself to be a Communist. If so, how could you now ever proclaim allegiance to the United States of America? The Communist party is a foreign agency dedicated to the violent overthrow of this country. You realize that incongruity? Don't you?"

Branko shook his head. "I no..."

"You came to Washington to create trouble, didn't you? You wanted to join with your comrades to foment mob action. You're an agitator," Tolson said.

"No. Please. I explain." Branko looked at his accuser for mercy. He had been with such men before. He saw no mercy in the man's eyes. They were empty. Tolson said nothing. Branko spoke quickly. His voice cracked. "I was young. The war ended. My country was a bad place. People were starving. People ate dogs. Children died. Flies on their bodies. The government was," he shook his head, "there was no government. Nothing was working. I was not working. Yes. I did sign with Communists. They made me member. I looked for hope. But I did not find it. In time, I know Communists wanted only pain. They wanted Serbia in pieces. The worst things were, the better for them to cut up country. I did not want this. After two years, I do nothing with them. I left. I traveled around. Job to job. Place to place. Then I find wife. With my brother, we start as circus performers. We are on the trapeze. Very good. Things are better. I forget war. I don't care about Communist."

"Then why do you carry the card? Why did you have it with you when we took you into custody?"

"I don't know. I kept some papers from old county. I wore it to say who I was. It is not big thing to be Communist in Europe. Not like here. I was stupid to keep."

"Maybe you needed it to join up with your comrades here in Washington. Right?"

Branko again shook his head. "No. No. No. I want to see these people because everyone said that they were to cause trouble. I do not want trouble. I want to help the war soldiers. I was one. We all fight same enemy. We fight Hun. These men are my real comrades. Not Communists."

"So what? What was your plan? We already know you have been meeting with John Pace. We know he has accepted you as a fellow traveler." Tolson smiled as he delivered the message.

"That is true," said Branko. "But I have no plan. I'm not coming to Washington until I meet a young woman who need help. I help her. To protect her. And she was coming here. So I came. She wanted to help veterans. So I did, too. I met with Communists to make sure they no cause trouble. But they are not trouble. They are not many. And they are not smart. They are…how you say? Pretend Communists. No worry about them. They will turn and run."

Tolson pursed his lips. "You may be right. This may turn out to be a flash in the pan, but we can take no chances with Communists. No matter how competent or incompetent. They are the sworn enemy of America. Do you understand?"

"I do. But I do not support them. I am a Serbian. I want to be American. I left my country, forever."

Tolson cocked his head. "Maybe…maybe not. We could have you sent back in the blink of an eye. You are an alien. You have been a card-carrying Communist. Do you know about deportation?"

Branko stayed silent. This was the word he did not want to hear. He could never go back. He was a wanted man in Serbia. About a year after his wife died, after he beat his brother, Dushan died. He didn't know what killed him. It may have been him. He didn't know for sure. But someone had told him they were after him. He got out of the country and did not want to return. Not just because he did not want to go to jail or worse, but because he wanted to start a new life in America. This was a country with problems, but he also sensed hope for the future. He liked the place. He wanted to stay. "What do you want? I will do anything?"

Tolson smiled. "All right. That sounds good. If you mean it."

"I do, Director. I do."

Tolson waited. And then he waited some more. Branko sweated. Tolson stared at him. Finally, Tolson tossed his head back and said, "You work for us now. You are totally under our command. You will do exactly as we say. You do that, and everything will be good for you. Who knows? Maybe we can forget this entire incident and pass on a good word to the immigration people. Life is full of possibilities for real Americans. For people who truly love and honor this country. What do you say, Mr. Brkovic?"

Branko thought, but not for long. "I work for you. What do I do?"

Tolson smiled. "Agent Carr. Please get Mr. Brkovic a cup of coffee. We have work to do."

In time, Carr returned with a cup of terrible-tasting coffee, but Branko told them it was excellent. He was working for them now, and he knew it. It didn't take long for them to come to the point. He was to return to Camp Glassford to meet again with the Communists. Ultimately, he was to either participate, or even assist them if necessary, in performing some illegal, dangerous, and newsworthy act of insurgency. He would make sure his masters at the Bureau knew precisely what was happening, and they would swoop in at just the right moment and arrest the lot of them. Branko assumed they would notify the newspapers before the raid to assure that the Bureau and Mr. Hoover received proper recognition for saving the city and the nation from the intolerable scourge of Communist agitators. In a way, none of this sounded terrible to Branko. If the Communists were blamed for causing trouble, it would not reflect upon the veterans. The Communists were separated from and hated by the veterans. There was no interaction so far as he could tell. So what if J. Edgar Hoover jumped into the limelight? As long as it did not result in a riot and no marchers or their family members were hurt, what difference did it make? This was all politics, like everything, everywhere.

LOG of Zak Newman

July 27, 1932 (local time): 11: 22 (Day 15 of time travel)

Emma is sick today. She has a fever, and her breathing is strained. We are concerned, but we don't want to bring in a doctor at this time. If we did and he decided she must go to a hospital, we would lose control over our schedule, and it would put a dagger into the heart of our mission. Ethan and I are taking turns ministering to her needs. At the moment, she is sleeping. I wouldn't say comfortably because her cough is chronic. Jack Travers has telephoned here, but we have decided not to inform him about her illness. Ethan thinks she may have picked up some kind of bug in the camp when she was helping the Sweeny family. I will keep a close eye on Emma.

Branko is gone. He returned late last night and went directly to bed. This morning he wouldn't talk about his time in jail. He told us that they let him go and that they only wanted to warn him. My guess is that he is only telling half the story. He was very concerned about Emma's health. He demanded that we watch over her. We told him we were not going anywhere today...that we would stay by her side. He looked intense when he left. I suspect he is up to something involving the Communists. I hope he is not looking for trouble. He's a man who can handle himself. Emma told us he saved her by beating the railroad guard over the head with a nightstick. Violence is part of him, and violence is the tool of the Communists. The Republicans promised "a chicken in every pot" in the 1928 election. But the American economic pot in 1932 has no chickens. It's filled only with stale promises and soggy hopes and dreams stewing above the flames of anger and despair. It is about to boil over — somehow, violence will erupt tomorrow here in

Washington with devastating effects. The American democracy will shut down unless something changes. We do need Governor Roosevelt to do something. He has the power to influence events. If he remains quiet, the future and history is in our hands alone.

But Emma is sick, and Ethan and I are becoming more impotent each day. We have already put the spotlight upon us. J. Edgar Hoover has us in his sights. I think Jack Travers spun a good tale to the Bureau of Investigation and used his political connections to get us free. But I don't think it's out of his love for us. I think he is just protecting his sweet Emma's brother and friend. I can't say I dislike the man, even though he's a smooth-talking womanizer. I can't say I like him either. Somehow, he doesn't fit. What the heck is he doing with us? I guess it's Emma. I can't blame him. But I don't like that at all. But she's a woman now — always making her way — "her way." I hope we will remain best friends when this is all over.

End 07-27-32

-Chapter XVI-

Fever Pitch

The next day, in the early morning of July 28, 1932, the phone rang in the time travelers' basement apartment. Ethan answered. "This is Jack Travers. How is Emma?"

"She's still sick, Jack. She had a bad night."

"Can I speak with her?"

"No. I don't think so. She's sleeping now."

There was a pause. "I understand. Then I'll tell you. I'm sorry to say that Mrs. Roosevelt has discussed Emma's idea with her husband, but he has decided only to take it under advisement at this time."

"What does that mean, Jack...in English?"

Again, a pause. "It means forget about it. It's not going to happen. I think it's too late anyway. Things are moving fast now. I'm in the midst of it. I just heard. They're going to clear out Camp Glassford today. Stay away from here today, Ethan. And take care of Emma. I'll stop by later to check on her. Call the doctor today. Get her to Dr. Archer, Ethan. Do you still have his information?"

Ethan rummaged through his shirt pocket and found the scrap of paper. "I have it, Jack. Don't worry, she'll be fine."

"All right, goodbye. I'll call back."

Ethan hung up the receiver and stared at the phone, wondering what they would do.

"Who was that?" A faint voice called from the bedroom.

Ethan entered Emma's room. "Sis, you're up." He looked at the bed, which appeared to be wet with sweat.

Emma lifted herself on her elbow. "Don't call me 'Sis,'" she said, managing a small smile.

"Sorry, Emma," he said. "That was Jack. He was calling to check on you."

She nodded, her eyes closing and opening as if she was drugged. "What else...?"

Ethan stumbled and said nothing. Just then, Zak entered the room. He asked about Emma, but she did not reply. Instead, she wondered, "What else did he say?"

"He said things are getting worse at Camp Glassford. And...he said your idea's a no-go. Mr. Roosevelt is 'taking it under advisement.' That means he will do nothing."

Emma was visibly agitated and upset. "They're all in danger. Where is Branko?"

"Please settle down, Emma. Branko is a big boy. He's fine. He's gone out for a while."

"And where is Jack? I need him. Where is he?" Her voice was weak.

"Jack is downtown. I just told you. He's reporting for the Roosevelts."

"Ethan. I'm sick. Help me. Please." She coughed violently for at least twenty seconds, and this time she brought up blood. The red sputum splattered on the white sheet. Dropping her head down into the pillow, she appeared to pass out.

"Emma..." Ethan put his hand on her forehead. He turned to Zak. "She's burning up, Zak. She's coughing up blood. Watch her. I've got to call the doctor."

Dr. Archer listened to the symptoms as Ethan described them and quickly decided. He told Ethan to put Emma into a taxi and immediately take her to St. Elizabeth's Hospital.

They dressed her and comforted her while they waited. She kept asking for Jack. The taxi arrived, and they battled their way across the city. Traffic was terrible. The cab driver pointed to the crowd of people flowing toward the downtown area where the marchers were staying. Police sirens filled the air, and police cars heading downtown dashed in and out of traffic. The evacuation was on. At every corner, policemen directed cars and people away from the action. The taxi was forced to cross the Anacostia River upstream of Camp Marks. Once on the other side, they made good time getting to the hospital, located atop a hill overlooking the city, just southwest of Camp Marks. At the hospital, the taxi stopped, and Ethan ran into the gatehouse. In a few minutes, he returned with a map in his hand.

"We're going to this one," he pointed on the map, "next to Building J."

"OK, Mack," said the driver, wheeling onto the winding road. "Say...she's not a nutcase, is she?"

"What?" said Ethan, who had only been half-listening.

"This place is an insane asylum."

"No. No. She's going to the tuberculosis area. Let's go."

The driver got the idea, and the taxi wound through the hospital lands, which to Ethan looked more like those of an eastern university than a mental hospital. They passed building after building until they finally broke out of the tree line and reached the southwest corner of the massive campus. The taxi pulled up in front of the brick structure bearing a sign that read *Admissions*. Emma was not able to walk into the building by herself. While Ethan paid the driver, Zak carried her like a baby into the large red brick building trimmed in limestone. Except for her incessant coughing, Emma sat quietly, almost asleep, while they waited in the lobby. Ethan could tell that every breath she took was painful. An attendant arrived. He placed her into a wheelchair and wheeled her away.

After they filled out some paperwork, they were told by a clerk to wait for the doctor. They waited. In about half an hour, the doctor arrived, and they moved to a nearby consulting room. The gray-haired physician introduced himself. He looked at the taller of the two visitors.

"You're Ethan."

"Yes."

"I see the resemblance. I've examined your sister. As is our standard procedure, she will be taking a blood test. And a fluoroscope. But even without seeing the results, I can tell you she has tuberculosis. Fairly serious case, I would add."

"Will she be all right?" asked Ethan.

"Time will tell," said the doctor. "She will need to be

isolated, and we will see. She needs bed rest, a proper diet, fresh air, and vitamins. However, she is young and otherwise in good health. Possibly her immune system has somehow been compromised. We would work to rebuild that. But it is too early to tell. I should warn you that this is a deadly disease. Your sister is at great risk."

"When will she get better?" asked Ethan.

"In time, son. Usually, those who will recover do so within six to eight months."

Ethan looked at Zak. They realized they were all in deep trouble.

"And we will have to test you two also. Since you have been near her, in close quarters, you may also have the disease. We'll give you a skin test, and you will have to return in a couple of days to have it read. Understood?"

They nodded.

"Also, you will not be able to see your sister while she is confined to the sanatorium."

"Not at all?" asked Ethan.

"No visits. Sorry."

Ethan looked at Zak. The doctor left. A nurse replaced him, and she administered the skin tests on the time travelers. They agreed to return in two days. They were told they would have to leave and were escorted out of the building. They sat on a bench in front and waited for another taxi to take them home. Their conversation was in sign language.

"We have a big problem, Zak. We may have to leave Emma," said Ethan.

"*For six months?*"

Ethan shrugged his shoulders. "This is serious, Zak. People die from tuberculosis. It looks like they have no idea how to treat it other than hoping it will go away."

"*Maybe it was a mistake to come here. Maybe we should have made a break for Mystic Heights. We could return there and be back in 2032 in no time. The TimeTravelle cycles every twelve hours. Maybe we should bust her out of this place,*" signed Zak.

"I don't know. They can make her comfortable. Maybe

deal with her fever and pain. In the meantime, we can get a plan going."

"*Right. We're real good with plans,*" said Zak. "*Our planning for this whole trip has been a bust. This thing with Emma is terrible. She must have picked it up in the camp.*"

"Who knows? We came here from a hundred years later. We're like lambs to the slaughter as far as these old diseases are concerned. We never thought about that. Maybe we could have brought medicine."

"*That would be a pretty big medicine bag. This world is filled with diseases. We've been lucky so far. Until now.*"

"We can't even see her now. We have to get something going soon. Otherwise, she may be trapped here in 1932."

They stopped their sign language conversation and looked out into the vast wooded complex of buildings, roads, and paths. Ethan's thoughts ran wild. But foremost in his mind was telling their father that Emma had been left behind.

Branko was in the midst of the action, downtown on Pennsylvania Avenue. He had joined up with the Communists early in the morning. Somehow, they knew that the eviction would begin today. By 10 a.m., the entire area was roped off and cleared by police. Commander Waters, the veterans' leader, had been called there to assist in a staged and orderly removal of his troops over the next several days. The area was quickly filling with people: veterans from other billets, spectators, and even politicians. As Branko watched, he stroked his mustache and contemplated. What was this man Waters going to say to all these people? Was he going to fire them up? Or would he calm them down? Branko hoped for the latter because he knew the Communists were in their element today. It was a perfect time to light a match. The veterans were desperate at the end of their ropes, dangling above oblivion. It reminded him of his wartime experiences. Why would men choose to charge into a hail of machine-gun bullets? It made no sense, yet men repeatedly did it with the same result. They did it for four years straight, and ten million soldiers died. They climbed out of their rat-infested, slime-filled trenches and ran toward certain death. These men in this crowd were those same men, veterans of that conflict. They might do it again.

Walter Waters, a U.S. Army sergeant in that great conflict, asked his men to work with Police Chief Glassford, but the crowd was not buying it. The men shouted that they wanted their bonus. More men showed up, swelling the ranks. Branko suspected his Communist buddies had put out the word to Camp Marks and the other billets that men were needed downtown. In any event, thousands of men were flooding the area. Waters continued to make his case for calmness until he was handed an envelope. He opened it and read it. Branko could see the man's entire face change. Waters read the order from Glassford aloud that demanded the immediate evacuation of all the veterans in the area. The buildings that housed the veterans were to be immediately demolished. "It's a double-cross," said Waters. "It's a double-cross."

Immediately after that pronouncement, government agents in the crowd, including Chief Glassford, announced they would begin clearing out the old Armory Building, the current home of about sixteen hundred former soldiers. Angry men shouted at the enforcers but took no action. As they stood their ground, Branko did nothing either. He looked around and recognized many Communists in the crowd. They were not grouped together, but they were there, watching.

Veterans left the building slowly. Some went back in to grab a few meager belongings but left without fighting. After about two hours, almost everyone was out of the abandoned building. Branko was pleased that nothing yet had happened. He knew what J. Edgar Hoover wanted. The director wanted the opportunity to be the hero. But his desire did not extend to being in the line of fire.

Then there was a groundswell of noise behind him. He felt the pressure of human bodies pushing him into the police rope. Someone shoved him onto the ground and stepped on him, driving him into the construction debris. In pain, he looked up and saw several men carrying an American flag, unfurled, as if in a battle charge. They had broken through the police lines. Others followed. Immediately, four or five cops moved in. One of them grabbed the flag. He was hit on the head with a lead pipe by a protester. It was hard to tell, but Branko thought the perpetrator might be one of the Communists.

Bricks and rocks began to fly out of the crowd, pummeling the police. The cops, without battle gear, white-shirted and wearing black ties and neat caps atop their heads, looked like angry businessmen as they retaliated, swinging their nightsticks wildly at any nearby head. Branko kept his head low and covered it with his hands as he watched the melee. A cop took a brick to his head and went down immediately. Other cops fell to the ground as they endured a hail of missiles. Wounded policemen were carried away. The Serbian was familiar with this scene. He was immediately mentally transported to his home country in 1915 during the Bloody Christmas, the Serbian army in retreat from the Austrians, beaten and struggling to reach the Albanian mountains. Branko, at that time a young lad of fifteen, saw plenty of hand-to-hand combat that winter. Another head cracked loudly, bringing him back to reality.

Chief Glassford popped into view not more than fifty feet from Branko. He mounted a pile of bricks and stood tall until a brickbat hit him in the chest. He recovered. "Come on, boys. Let's call an armistice for lunch." Incredibly, the men dropped their bricks, pipes, and clubs and cheered. The fighting stopped. Never in all the battles Branko had experienced, had the action just stopped. It was as if a referee had signaled the end of a football game. Branko shook his head. Glassford was a courageous man. The Serbian rose slowly as he brushed off the dust and dirt and walked away from the scene. Ambulances arrived to remove the wounded. The first battle of the war was over. The police line was re-established. It was a stalemate, just like the World War, thought Branko.

Branko couldn't find any of his Communist comrades. The Red camp was several blocks away. He suspected those men ran away from the action. He walked to a nearby drugstore, used the washroom, bought a bottle of soda, and placed a call to Special Agent Tolson to report the morning events. Their conversation was stilted. Tolson made him repeat the story twice. Branko promised him that he was in the middle of the action and that he would report any further developments. Tolson asked him if the Communists were involved. Branko said he didn't think so. Should he return to the Red camp? Tolson said no. "Stay with the eviction." Overall, Tolson seemed disappointed with the news. Then, like a schoolteacher, he reminded Branko of his responsibility to the Bureau. Deferentially, Branko pledged allegiance and hung up.

As he exited the phone booth, he muttered "generals," followed by several Serbian swear words. Once outside, he bought a hot dog from a street vendor, who was making a killing that day. Branko loved American hot dogs. He sat on the curb, watched the milling crowd's swishing feet and legs, and ate his lunch. At his location, one block from the United States Capitol Building, the mass of people continued to grow. Vacationers, visitors, and government workers gathered to watch. The day evolved and became a holiday of public violence and spectacle. Word was out that the drawbridge to Anacostia was open, and veterans from Camp Marks were streaming into the area. Branko thought there might be five thousand people as he looked across the street. He had a front-row seat at the "Battle of Pennsylvania Avenue." He sensed the real action was coming. An hour later, it began.

Branko was at the front. He stood at the base of a half-demolished four-story concrete and brick warehouse building. Veterans filled its innards, milling about like rats in a maze. Something was happening. He saw Chief Glassford with two other policemen running toward the building. Again the crowd surged, this time carrying

Branko forward. Things were getting out of control. The three-quarter-inch rope that separated the former soldiers from the cops was breached. Men flooded in. Angry shouts filled the air as Glassford climbed a stair leading to the second floor of the building. Above and below him, men shouted in anger. Debris dropped down from above. Bricks flew in from the crowd. Someone grabbed one of the cops and tossed him to the ground.

A garbage can from the third floor landed nearby and vomited its contents. A brick hit another cop. A man as large and quick as a bear stole a nightstick from the downed cop and beat him with it. More bricks hit the cops and peppered the turf around them. The first cop, his head bloodied from the beating, drew his pistol, aimed, and fired twice. At the sound of gunshots, the soldiers fell to the ground. This was very real now. People were dying. For sure, a riot will ensue. And Branko was dead center in the middle of it. His gut told him that he might be next.

Someone shouted, "Stop that shooting!" It was the police chief. The wounded cop, still on the ground and holding the smoking gun, now pointed it at his boss. He wore a crazed look. For a second, Branko thought that Glassford was next. But it was over. The cop laid down his gun.

The smell of gunpowder in the air reminded everyone of the war. Nobody wanted this. It had moved beyond politics, protesting, and jeers. One veteran had died instantly, and another was mortally wounded. More ambulances arrived and carried away the injured policemen and the two veterans. But there was no riot. The dangerous dance between the police and the protestors was over for the moment. Branko wondered if anyone in the government was thinking. None of this had to happen. In time, these men would just fade away like the old soldiers that they were. If they had food in their stomachs, they would have no fire in their bellies. They had been brought to action today by the eviction deadlines. A strangely American word, he thought, "deadline." Afterward, he reported back to Agent Tolson, telling him of the violence; nothing was organized or sustained, and nothing was Communist-inspired. As far as he knew, the Reds were still holed up with John Pace over on D Street. Tolson was disappointed. Branko vowed to continue his role as the Bureau spy.

Sirens wailed nearby, distorting his hearing. He hung up the phone, stayed in the booth, and cried quietly, burying his head into a corner so no one could see. He was overcome with visions of the Bloody Christmas in Serbia in 1915.

-Chapter XVII-

Call Out the Cavalry

Standing shoulder to shoulder with thousands of other onlookers on the north side of Pennsylvania Avenue, Jack Travers contemplated the future. After the violent melee a few hours earlier, the street was cleared by the police, and the spectators had been herded back into the approved viewing area. Veterans across the street milled about, some eating, some talking, others watching the watchers, everyone playing a part in this participatory theater. The first battles were over. The dead and the wounded had been removed. Maybe the veterans thought this was just another stalemate, something that would continue to grind on relentlessly without resolution, like the war in France.

Today, in fascination and anticipation, the people of Washington were drawn to this location. Travers wondered if anyone in the crowd remembered a similar group of interested bystanders who had gathered seventy-one years earlier at Manassas, just thirty miles west of the city. In 1861, hundreds of spectators rode out of the city in carriages and watched from the sidelines while sixty thousand soldiers readied themselves for battle. Bull Run, the first significant engagement of the Civil War, was a terrifying event filled with blood, guts, death, and dismemberment. The battle was an overture to the horrific four-year drama that would follow. On that day, five thousand men were wounded or killed. The spectators, who had brought picnic lunches and beer, soon panicked and ran for their lives. Travers wondered: What had they expected? What did the people surrounding him now expect? Nothing good would come of this. This was not entertainment.

Travers knew Chief Pelham Glassford. The head cop of

Washington, D.C., had been the youngest American field grade brigadier general in the World War. He understood people in conflict. For the past six months, he managed the "tourists," as he called them, the hunger marchers, Communists, war veterans, and unemployed. They came. They protested. They marched. And they left. He had dealt with them humanely, even providing food and shelter for some. This was, after all, the Great Depression. And Washington, D.C., was the capital of the nation. The city was a twentieth-century Roman Forum, and Glassford was the centurion in charge of the *cohortes urbanae.* The people gathered to air their opinions and complain. Glassford and his police force kept them in line but let them squawk. However, in the minds of the higher powers in Washington, Chief Glassford was just a cop who worked for the district. He had handled his job well, but the national leaders were nervous. Some thought he coddled the protestors, and some feared insurrection. It was time to solve the problem for good, so they ordered their soldiers to mobilize.

Unlike Glassford, a civil servant, General Douglas MacArthur marched to the drumbeat of the nation's leader, President Herbert Hoover. Unfortunately for his civilian superior, MacArthur was known to interpret his marching orders liberally. He was a man who always wanted to get the job done correctly and completely, no matter what. In charge of the troops surrounding the city, he was assisted by his aide, Major Dwight D. Eisenhower and Major George S. Patton Jr. All had fought in the big war with Glassford and the tens of thousands of veterans who now squatted in Washington. It was a strange and combustive gathering of former brothers-in-arms.

Travers and Glassford had something in common. Chief Glassford, the boss of the local cops and a champion of the common man, was also known to enjoy the company of refined gentlemen and ladies. He understood Travers' position within the Roosevelt campaign and had extended certain privileges to him. They both loved the arts, with Glassford already achieving some notoriety as an accomplished artist. Travers had dined with him several times, and they enjoyed their lively discussions about art, politics, and the country's future. Engaging, knowledgeable, and talented, Pelham Glassford was a complicated, sensitive, and intelligent man in his actions and thoughts.

A few hours ago, Glassford had almost single-handedly tamed the potential riot, but now that pot began to boil again. The chief roared past the crowd on his blue motorcycle and drove into the billet area. He was quickly surrounded by his officers. Travers followed him on foot. About twenty feet away and behind a rope, Jack Travers waved and shouted at Glassford. The head cop spotted him and authorized his access across the police line.

"Jack," said Glassford. He stood tall at six-foot-four and looked like a handsome, Hollywood version of a crime fighter. "Busy now. Very busy."

"Any news?" asked Travers.

Glassford swung his head around, surveying the situation. "I'll tell you what I told the boys. General MacArthur thinks he's back in France, full-dress uniform, ribbons, boots, and all. He's ready for the photographers. And his troops will be here shortly. If you know any of these vets, tell them to evacuate now. This is serious, Jack. It's out of my hands."

"Are they going to clear them out?"

"This is the Army, Jack. They operate under a different set of rules. Martial law. Now, you have to go. I've got work to do. This could turn into a mess." Ignoring Jack's next question, Glassford ran back to his motorcycle and drove away, kicking up a cloud of dust and stones.

Jack was moved quickly back to the other side of the rope that separated the civilians from the "mob," as President Hoover later called them. Travers rejoined the crowd of young mothers in summer dresses guarding their baby carriages, businessmen, school kids, and other rubberneckers lining the street. Glassford's men did a great job of separating the combatants from the spectators. It was the quiet before the storm.

Travers heard the faint, distant rumble of trucks rolling and horses trotting on hard pavement, not loud at first but still ominous. People looked down Pennsylvania Avenue toward the White House. In the distance, he saw something significant moving onto the street. Slowly, a dark, disciplined mass of horse and human flesh approached. When the first wave of cavalrymen reached Travers' location, the crowd was cheering as if it was a parade, but Travers knew better. Two hundred soldiers on horses sat tall in the saddle, their sabers ready for action. The horse soldiers were impressive and frightening, wearing their Stetson campaign hats, strapped with bandoliers and carbines.

Major Patton led his troops in tight formation. Horses snorted. The clacking of their steel shoes on the pavement was deafening. A light wind carried the atmosphere of combat into the crowd. The sweating horseflesh and fresh manure baking on hot pavement added a primitive olfactory dimension to the threat. Behind the rows and rows of horsemen, trucks loaded with tanks and mobile machine guns lumbered on. Barely visible to Travers, at the rear, the lines of four hundred infantrymen in full battle gear marched steadily toward Camp Glassford.

Travers looked at those in the crowd surrounding him. Protective senses activated, anxious mothers pushed their baby carriages away from the action. Innocent youngsters on summer break stood wide-eyed, captivated by the pageantry of the soldiers on horses. Three nearby men laughed and joked, apparently ignorant of the reality of the situation. He looked back at the street. Infantrymen marched before him. He looked to his right and saw staff cars moving behind the foot soldiers. In the rear seat of the lead car, the jaw-jutting commander, General Douglas MacArthur, in full military dress, sat proud and tall.

Then, abruptly, the line of men and machines stopped. On command, the soldiers pivoted neatly to face the veterans. They fixed bayonets on their rifles and donned gas masks, ready. Jack Travers knew this was the beginning of the end. In command of the troops, an officer on foot shouted a demand to the disjointed potential combatants milling about in Camp Glassford. The veterans stopped all activity and froze, probably straining to hear or understand his words. An order, unintelligible to the crowd or to the veterans, was shouted out by the officer. A few seconds passed before all hell broke loose. The soldiers pulled out gas grenades and threw them at the veterans. They bounced across the grass like hot grounders at Griffith Stadium, spewing out choking clouds of disabling gas.

For the vets, it was a replay of the killing fields of France. In desperation, they grabbed their handkerchiefs and held them over their faces. The gas choked their lungs and stung their eyes. Some picked up the grenades and valiantly tossed them back at the soldiers. But waves of infantrymen wearing protective gas masks and carrying bayonet-tipped rifles overwhelmed them, rushing past the fleeing or doubled-over and incapacitated veterans. The militia entered the buildings and flooded the interiors with tear gas. Anyone not wearing a mask could not survive in this environment. In short order, the veterans blindly stumbled away from the pain, prodded by the bayonets of the ground troops and the poundings from the flat sides of the cavalrymen's sabers.

The mounted military methodically drove the veterans south, away from the Capitol, and the armored cavalry struck next. Tanks rattled and rumbled, driving ahead through the smoke crushing everything in their paths as soldiers ran from shack to shack, setting fire to the remains of the pitiful Hooverville. The cardboard, wood, and fabric make-believe homes burned quickly, creating a whirlwind of flame, smoke, and gas. Camp Glassford, now vacated, was burning.

The ever-expanding gas clouds soon threatened those spectators who watched the action from the other side of Pennsylvania Avenue. The wind was blowing the wrong way that day, directly into their faces. Now they became participants in the action. People screamed, choked, and ran. Then, incredibly and almost surrealistically, the soldiers on horseback, wearing gas masks, attacked the bystanders. The former spectators endured the same fate as the veterans had.

Behind him, women with baby carriages, now in a panic, pushed them haphazardly. One woman lost control, and her carriage tipped over. She grabbed her infant from the ground, abandoned the pram, and continued running away from the soldiers.

This was hell, thought Jack Travers. He was on the run as horsemen closed in on him. Soldiers whooped with war cries. Over his shoulder, a hairy, dark hulk filled his vision. The noise was deafening. The animal's head was only inches from his, and its noisy, hot, wet breath filled him with fear. He saw teeth, leather, a foaming nostril, and one big eye on a black horsehair backdrop. He felt the whack of the flat side of a swinging saber pound into his right shoulder, and he went down. In passing, the tip of the soldier's blade nicked his neck. Travers hit the ground hard.

Dazed and almost afraid to do so, he reached up and felt the wetness of his own blood flowing. He lifted his head and looked around, absorbing the nightmare. It was like the Battle of Little Bighorn, except the soldiers were winning: the sabers slapping home, the people screaming, and clouds of poisonous gas bringing everyone to their knees. But they kept moving, as did Jack Travers.

He got up, staggered on, and then he ran. Keep moving away from the battleground. Keep moving, he told himself. His lungs screamed with pain.

Sirens wailed, and tanks rumbled and clanked across the pavement. Jack stopped running. He looked back at what had been Camp Glassford. Flames and smoke climbed high into the sky, and above the Washington Monument towered in the distance.

For the moment, the citizens of Washington were left alone to lick their wounds, soak their eyes with wet handkerchiefs, and hold their heads in despair. The soldiers had moved away to attack the veterans. Around him, hundreds ministered to themselves and their families. Jack did this for many minutes, verifying that all his parts were still attached. He sat and put his middle finger onto his neck wound. It was a surface wound. His hands shook as he lit a cigarette and took a deep drag. The nicotine helped dull the pain. But nothing could stop the sights and sounds of the madness before him. The government's army attacked its own citizens in Washington, D.C., the nation's capital. He had known this was coming, but the reality of the event was far more painful than he anticipated. Physically, emotionally, and philosophically, he was a beaten man.

He stumbled out of the area and found a phone booth. He gave the operator the number of Emma's apartment. He wanted to talk with her. He wanted to hear her voice. But the phone kept ringing without an answer until the call was interrupted and the line went dead. "Emma..." Travers found himself talking to himself. Adrenaline slowly moved back to wherever it came from. His body and mind were racked with pain.

He staggered out of the phone booth and moved on, staying away from the action. Several blocks later, he found his car where he had parked it hours ago. It felt good to sit in the leather seat, holding the steering wheel in his hands, enjoying the calm. With the top up, it was quiet in the car. He reached into the glove compartment, found his silver flask, and took a slug. The booze ignited his gas-attacked throat, but he needed it. He took one more drink for the road, feeling at least half-human now. Psychologically, his other half lay on the ground near Pennsylvania Avenue. He started the car and drove off slowly with no destination in mind.

Almost without thought, he switched on the radio. The airwaves were filled with the story of the attack on the marchers. He learned that the veterans were being driven south. Thousands of men were seen running across the drawbridge over the Anacostia River, racing to the safety of Camp Marks. At this moment, after having secured Camp Glassford's evacuation, the soldiers were moving on toward the Communist positions. Travers knew those men would get the same treatment, probably worse. The old World War veterans weren't really the enemy. They were just a nuisance and an embarrassment to President Hoover. Fifteen years earlier, those men would have been considered brothers. But the Communists would be regarded as the enemy in the wild eyes of soldiers tasting blood for the first time in their young military careers. Attacking Communists would justify today's dubious action.

However, the enemy was not to be found. The Reds fled before the soldiers arrived. Travers drove aimlessly around the city as the action continued, and the radio voice told the story. *"Informed sources say that the evacuation mission executed by the military will terminate at the 11th Street drawbridge."*

Jack Travers laughed at the reporter, knowing the great General MacArthur would take this mission to its logical end. President Hoover's mistake was to think he could control men at war, even if that war was on his doorstep. Travers shouted at the radio voice, "Tell that to MacArthur!" He took another swig of booze before tossing the flask back into the dash and closing the glove box.

-Chapter XVIII-

The Walking Wounded

Ethan and Zak stood outside their apartment door. Ethan fumbled with the key. Inside, the phone was ringing.

"*That might be the hospital*," said Zak. But Ethan wasn't looking at him, so he didn't see him talk.

Ethan finally got the key into the lock and opened the door. He raced for the phone, but it stopped ringing before he could lift the receiver. "Damn," he said. "Think we should call the hospital? Maybe something is wrong." Ethan looked at Zak for guidance. His mind was numbed by the thought of his sister's illness.

"*No. They'll call again if it's something important. Forget it. We've got to think about freeing Emma.*"

For the next hour, they discussed possible approaches to bust Emma free, but all of them required the use of a car. They would have to bring Jack Travers into the plot unless they could find an unusually cooperative cabbie who didn't mind a little law-breaking. This was something they wanted to avoid. Somehow they had to get her out and immediately head back to Mystic Heights. Emma's condition would only worsen if she attempted to ride the rails or take a passenger train back. With transfers, it was a two-day trip. They had to get her back to the year 2032, where they hoped that doctors could quickly cure her tuberculosis. They knew nothing about this disease except that it was unheard of in their time and place.

"If we can just get her back quickly, I'm sure we can make her well, Zak."

"*Right*," Zak said. And then, after thinking a moment, he signed: "*Airplane. Remember that sight-seeing plane we saw flying above the Justice Department building... the Potomac Flying Service. Maybe they can fly us back to*

Mystic Heights."

Ethan brightened. "That's an idea. That's a good idea."

Behind them, the door to the apartment opened, and Branko stumbled in. He held a bloody handkerchief to his head. Both time travelers grabbed him and walked him to the sofa. He sat down. Ethan looked at him. His face had open cuts, and his clothes were dirty. His shirt was ripped.

"What happened, Branko?" asked Ethan.

"Soldiers. The Army got us at Camp Glassford. I did nothing. No one did anything. They gassed us. It was horrible. Soldiers attack their own men. Terrible."

"Are you hurt?"

Branko looked up. "No. I just need to be clean. We must go to Camp Marks. We must tell them to leave. Army will not stop. I see the look of the men. They will kill if necessary. Kill own people." He dropped his head and then looked into his handkerchief, tossing it to the ground. "How is Emma? Is she sleeping?"

Ethan cleared his throat. "We took her to the hospital, Branko. I'm afraid she is very ill...tuberculosis."

Branko scowled. "Everything I touch..." he muttered to himself.

"What?"

"Nothing. Tell me about Emma. Please."

They explained how they had taken her to the hospital and gave him all the details, including that it might take months for her to get better. Branko was devastated. He got up and went to the bathroom while Zak and Ethan waited. Not much was said. In a few minutes, he came out, clad only in his underwear.

"I need to lie down," he said as he limped into the bedroom. They heard him flop onto the bed.

"He looked bad. I guess the battle has begun. And Branko is one of the first casualties," signed Zak.

"He's right about one thing," said Ethan.

Zak waited for an explanation.

"We need to get to Camp Marks. We need to prevent the massacre."

"*Or die trying....*" Zak made a face and shrugged his shoulders.

Emma awoke. For a moment, she had no idea where she was. Then she remembered that she had been taken to a hospital. But where were Ethan and Zak? Why was she alone? The hospital room was small and dark except for a dim lamp over the door. The bed faced a panel of windows, some of which were open. She sensed the hot, muggy night air and heard boat whistles in the distance. Maybe she was near the river. She gathered her strength and lifted her head off the pillow, and the view was startling. The sky was glowing orange. For a moment, she thought her illness was affecting her mind. But then she saw the illuminated buildings and monuments floating above an orange cloud of smoke. Flames from an enormous fire leaped into the air near the Capitol. Something was terribly wrong.

Her fever subsided. She tried to get out of bed, but the effort caused her to cough. A metal bottle and a glass were on the side table. She attempted to pour the water into the glass. Some went in; most ended up on the table. But she drank, and she felt better.

For some time, she just sat, trying to get her bearings. She was alone, and she listened carefully. Everything was quiet. The door to the room was open. Slowly, she dragged herself to the doorway. Her room was at the end of the long corridor. Standing in her hospital gown, naked underneath, she watched silently. Cooler air funneled up her legs, awakening concerns of modesty. She was confused. About a hundred feet distant, she saw a nurse dressed in white sitting at a desk in the corridor, reading something. Emma receded and sat on the edge of the bed. She shook her head to clear her mind.

She remembered a doctor examining her and the word "tuberculosis." This had frightened her. The mere thought of the word took her back to old movie scenes of hospital wards full of white metal beds with white sheets and street urchin youngsters coughing. The kids would tell each other not to worry. Everything would be all right. And then one of their little friends would die. And the ward would grow silent as the body of little "Jimmy" or "Shorty," completely covered with a white sheet, would slowly be rolled out of the room before the crying eyes of the other innocent children struck down with the deadly disease. Fiction and reality meshed. Her 1930s movie memories blended with the present; she was the victim now. She was going to die.

Maybe the sound of distant sirens seeping through the window screens focused her mind. Or the ominous flames of a burning city appearing in the distance. She knew today was the day of the massacre. The marchers had been routed. Mrs. Roosevelt did not convince her husband to think beyond election strategy, Franklin Roosevelt didn't take the risk, and President Hoover had finally jumped over the political cliff. Ironically, it happened just as was written in the usually unreliable 2032 official compilation of the past, *The History*. Even a broken clock is correct twice a day, she thought.

She looked around for her clothes and found them in a locker. Quietly, stifling her urge to cough, she slipped into her light green shirt, which smelled of dried sweat, some smelly underwear, her plaid skirt, a pair of white socks, and white buck shoes. Ethan and Zak did a decent job dressing her on the fly, except she was braless. Oh, well, she thought, there goes the mystery. The flat heels of her sensible shoes were most important. She had made the decision to break out of her confinement. She had to get to the Sweeny family. She had no idea of the time of day and had only pieced together a hint of her location, but she knew the climax of the military action would happen late at night on the 28th of July. There was a clock on the wall that read 8:39. Unless they had drugged her, today was the 28th. There was still time.

She went to the window and looked out. She was on the first floor. It was too dark to know what was outside. The rising moon's light allowed her to make out a nearby road, which appeared to encircle the building. Quietly, she lifted the window until it was completely open. The sill was at waist height, and if she could remove the screen, she could crawl out. She tested it by pushing on it. It didn't move; she looked for locking devices but saw none. The metal screening was a heavy gauge intended to contain people like her who dreamed of escape. She returned to the open door and looked around the edge of the door frame. She waited. The nurse fumbled with some papers; her white cap and face were illuminated by the bright light of a green glass desk lamp. After a few minutes, she left her desk and walked up the corridor and out of sight.

It was now or never. Tiptoeing along the corridor, Emma fought off dizziness and fear. Finally, she slipped behind the desk. She froze and listened, fearing the nurse might return. The only sounds were those of her labored breathing.

She found a pair of scissors and a letter opener in the top desk drawer. Grabbing both, she closed the drawer and quickly but quietly made her way to her room. As she darted in, she glanced back. The nurse returned. Emma leaned against the inside door jamb, her breaths echoing in her ears. She rested and listened. The nurse was making a telephone call. It was time to move into action.

She rushed across the room and immediately attacked the window screen. Using the letter opener to puncture the mesh, she inserted the scissors and cut the material. In less than a minute, her doorway to freedom was complete. She stood on a chair, pushed open the flap of screening, and hung her leg out. Weakened by her illness, every muscle strained as she contorted her body to escape. Finally, grasping the windowsill, she pushed away and dropped to the ground, landing in the soft grass. She stood perfectly still, listening, but heard nothing but the sounds of frogs and crickets. Without looking back, she pranced away from the building.

After crossing the road, she got her bearings and headed for the city of Washington in the distance. The Anacostia River lay ahead at the bottom of a long, gentle slope leading to freedom.

Jack held his woman in his arms and comforted her in his dream world. She smiled and gently squeezed his hand, and they kissed. Slowly, he broke free into reality as he awakened from a deep sleep. His head, still filled with thoughts of Emma, rested on the steering wheel. He reached back and gingerly touched his saber wound. Reality had returned. He hoped that Ethan and Zak had followed his advice and brought her to the doctor. She would be all right. At least she wasn't involved with the melee and the gassing. In her condition, the tear gas fumes would have killed her. He remembered the women and children who had coughed and gagged during the attack just a few minutes ago. But it wasn't a few minutes; it had been hours. He had parked his car on a quiet street, stopped the engine, drank the remainder of the whiskey in his flask, and then fell asleep. Now, it was dark, and his watch read 8:50. He started the car and drove away fast, heading for Emma's apartment.

Emma stumbled through the weeds and brush. Each second without hearing an alarm was a victory to her. She looked back. Except for a few street lamps, the hospital complex was dark and quiet. There was no sign of activity. The hospital building on the hill looked like a foreboding fortress in the moonlight. She exhaled and coughed in pain, tired but happy that she had escaped. As she advanced downhill, she moved onto farmland. All around her, green was growing. She hadn't seen a sight like this since their flight to 1963. Food was not produced in the world of 2032 in Mystic Heights; it simply arrived there from someplace else unknown to the residents. She liked the reality of this food, whatever it was. Her fever had returned, and sweat dripped down her forehead. She wiped her brow. The salty perspiration stung her eyes; she rubbed them and stared intently into the night. Her head was spinning, but she moved on.

Ahead, she saw the flames of the Hooverville burning brightly in the sky. Camp Glassford, she surmised. She paused to orient herself again. Unseen boats worked the Potomac River to her left, their navigation lights moving silently through the night quite a distance from her. Straight ahead, an airplane beacon revolved and reached out, rotating like a giant yellow arm. That could be Bolling Field, she thought. Beyond and to the right, the Washington Monument and the Capitol Building were visible. The fires in front of the Capitol flamed brightly while sirens screamed in the distance. It was a tragic but magnificent scene. The rigging lights on the masts of the sailing warship *Constitution* anchored at the Navy yard swayed gently. Nearby, the radio tower's blinking red warning lights flashed on and off. She knew the old ship was across the river from Camp Marks, so she searched for the veteran's camp, but all was dark in that direction. That was good news; nothing was burning yet. Each step became a struggle. The downhill nature of her course kept her going, along with her determination to save her friends from danger. As reflections of orange and yellow flames twinkled in the Anacostia River, a bright moon popped out from behind a cloud, revealing the way ahead. About a quarter-mile distant, she spied the road that paralleled the river, and beyond that, maybe twice the distance, an automobile cruised along, its headlights cutting a path through the night leading to the soldier's encampment. Not much longer, she thought.

Someone pounded on the door of the apartment. Ethan opened the door, and Travers entered quickly. "Where's Emma? How is she?"

Ethan smelled liquor on Travers' breath. "Jack. Have you been drinking?" Then he saw the blood that covered Jack's neck and shoulder. His suit was soaked in blood. "You're wounded."

He ignored Ethan's comment. "Is she all right? Did you

call the doctor?"

"She's in the hospital, Jack. Tuberculosis."

"Oh. No."

Branko staggered out of the bedroom, still in his underwear. He looked at the three. "We must go. We must. Mr. Travers. Please, drive me to camp."

"We're not going anywhere," said Travers, "until I talk to Emma." He removed his suit jacket and tossed the mess onto the floor. Then he walked to the phone and picked up the receiver. "Where is she, Ethan? What hospital?"

Ethan thought. His mind went blank. He looked at Zak, who signed to him. He told Travers: "She's at St. Elizabeth's."

Travers wasted no time having the operator connect him with the hospital. His words flew fast. "I don't know." Pause. "Who am I? Who is this? I want to speak to her."

"Jack..." said Ethan. He wanted to tell him that no one could speak to her.

"What? When?" He hung up the receiver and looked at the others with wide eyes of disbelief. "They say she escaped."

Chapter XIX

Night Terrors

As they rode south in Travers' car, Ethan and Jack debated. Should they go to the hospital, call the police, or go to Camp Marks. Finally, they agreed that unless Emma was totally out of her mind and lost, she escaped for one reason, to save Molly Sweeny and her children. Before they left, Jack Travers had made a call to someone "in the know" who could provide him with updated information. This person, whom Ethan assumed was in the government, told Travers that the camp would not be attacked that evening. General MacArthur had orders from the President not to cross the bridge and not to evacuate Camp Marks. Not tonight. But Ethan knew what he knew. July 28th was the day.

The marchers would riot and die tonight, and the American republic would disappear. Emma might be unable to stop the calamity, but she could warn the seven thousand residents of Camp Marks, including six hundred women and children. Given the proximity of St. Elizabeth's Hospital to the Anacostia River and the visibility of the fires still raging downtown, he convinced Jack that she would quickly figure it out and head to the camp. Ethan knew Branko would support this theory. He was a man who had experienced the violence of war firsthand. He wanted to stop the carnage. These men had suffered enough, and innocent women and children were in danger. Branko insisted that the government soldiers would go in for the kill tonight.

As they drove toward the 11th Street drawbridge, it was more peaceful. Active fires still lit the sky between them and the Capitol, but the cacophony of police sirens had died down. The sidewalks were filled with marchers returning to Camp Marks. Soldiers herded them, using their bayonets for emphasis when necessary. Jack followed a zigzag route through back streets that hadn't been closed, avoiding most of the crowds and the militia. Ethan guessed that the bulk of the military was massed west of them. The thousands of spectators, who had poured out to witness the events on Pennsylvania Avenue, were gone. Ethan suspected that they had come to understand that there were no spectators in a modern war. The noxious fumes of the gas grenades were weapons without discrimination.

Travers drove rapidly through the city, with Ethan riding shotgun and Zak and Branko in the rumble seat. The top was up on the Buick, and anyone seeing it shoot by at top speed might believe it to be an official's car. The marchers were not driving, and only a foolish civilian would be going anywhere on this night in Washington. It was far too dangerous. Ethan hung his elbow out the window, bracing himself as Travers cut and wove his way to the river. About two hundred yards from the drawbridge, they slowed.

Travers tossed his cigarette out the window and turned to talk to Ethan. "Let me do the talking. Open the glove box and remove the leather document cover." Travers reached into his shirt pocket, pulled out a key, and handed it to Ethan.

As they bounced along, Ethan struggled to open the box. It flipped down, and he removed Travers' now empty silver flask, grabbed the leather folder, and handed it to Jack. He didn't remove the nickel-plated .32 automatic that rested at the bottom of the box. Ethan looked up and gave Jack a questioning look.

"Put the booze back and lock it up, Ethan," said Jack.

Ethan locked the glove box without making a comment. He looked ahead. Two military cars and a troop truck were parked at the head of the bridge. To get Ethan's attention, Zak, who was riding high above in the rumble seat, tapped on the car's roof. In response, Ethan looked to his right. In the distance, formations of soldiers appeared to be marching toward them along the road that fronted the Navy yard. Behind the troops, tanks fired up. Their open-port engines abruptly broke the quiet of the evening. They coughed up clouds of exhaust, which were caught in the glow of the street lamps. Some tanks moved, clattering noisily across the concrete. The next battle was coming soon. The mechanized cavalry would reach the bridge in minutes.

The car bore down on the 11th Street drawbridge, and a khaki-clad soldier appeared in the headlights. He wore a .45 on his hip and a determined look. He stretched out both hands in front of him, ordering the car to stop. Travers braked, and the soldier came around the driver's side. Through the windshield, Ethan saw veterans lining both sides of the bridge. He sensed the camp population had been restocked. Additional thousands of men who had been routed out of Camp Glassford sought refuge tonight. Driven out like rats, they had found a temporary hiding place in the darkness of Camp Marks.

"Your business here, sir?" asked the young soldier. He quickly swung his flashlight beam around the inside of the car, then on Zak and Branko, and then returned it to Travers' face.

"If you don't mind, Sergeant..." said Travers as he handed the man his credentials.

The soldier dropped his light to view the identification and credentials. He studied them carefully and nodded. Apparently, he was comfortable with the presence of Jack Travers and the three others. "As you know, we have a situation here, sir. This is a military operation. We expect more trouble tonight. Why are you here?"

Travers looked at the man and spoke with assurance and urgency. "We need to get in and out as fast as possible. A woman on my staff was on special assignment in the camp. I was informed that she was seriously ill earlier in the day and could not leave the camp. I need to remove her to a hospital now. She is a niece of Mrs. Roosevelt." He nodded to his right. "This is her brother and two of her friends who have volunteered to assist me. May we please enter?"

The soldier seemed to think for a moment. He looked around, then back. "You'll have to do it pretty damn quick, Mr. Travers. As I said, this is a military operation. We cannot guarantee the safety of anyone."

"We know exactly where she is. And I have this." He pointed to the Buick's spotlight. "We'll find her. Now, may we?"

"Make it fast."

"Thanks." Travers didn't wait for any additional confirmation. He put the car in gear and drove across the drawbridge flipping on the windshield-mounted spotlight, aiming it to the left front. It cut through the night, catching the faces of the men shielding their eyes. He tapped his horn to clear a couple of others lingering on the roadway. Finally, they reached the other side. Ethan wondered about the intentions of the veterans who had been directed here from the downtown encampments. Did they think they could sleep along the riverbank or on the ridges above the camp? Before the new thousands of men arrived, Camp Marks was already a fully occupied jigsaw jumble of trash, debris, torn tents, and shaky shacks. There would be no room at this inn.

Once over the bridge, Zak jumped out of the car, moved quickly to the bridge railing, and sat atop it. He would remain in that location as a scout. If the troops began crossing the bridge, he would run to the Sweeny's hut to warn everyone. Ethan hoped the three of them could get in and out with Emma before any soldiers took action. Taking advantage of the moment, he stepped out of the car and onto its running board. Standing there, he hoped to maximize his ability to see and hear to find Emma and the Sweeny family. Jack put the car in gear, and it lurched ahead. Ethan braced himself and hung on. As they drove away across the dried mud flats of Camp Marks, Ethan looked back over his shoulder. He could make out the 11th Street drawbridge silhouetted against the skyline. Clouds of cigarette smoke rose above the groups of marchers who had gathered there after escaping the downtown attacks. The men bonded, smoked, talked, and nervously joked about the day's action. Probably most were discussing their narrow escapes at the battle of Camp Glassford just a few hours ago and comparing them to their wartime experiences in 1918. Now, the war had come home to America. As the car bounced along, Ethan swung around and looked ahead into the darkness. He wondered if the veterans realized they were now boxed into the Anacostia flats with no way out. The United States Army was marshaling its forces on the other side of the river, preparing to attack its own. Time was running out.

The Buick drove slowly through the city of forgotten vets. Travers played his spotlight back and forth, exposing a zombie force, masses of men, invisible in the blackness of the night, who lay in the shadows along the main road into the camp. To Ethan, it was maddening. Besides the Navy yard across the river and the distant orange glow of the fires destroying Camp Glassford, he couldn't see anything. Thousands of people were gathering in the dark, armies were massing nearby, and parts of the city were burning, yet it was relatively quiet. The mating calls of frogs in the shallows of the Anacostia filled the air. Somewhere, somebody was playing guitar and singing a ballad. The unintelligible voices of a large gathering of men at the river created a muffled, looping sonic background as they wafted over the steamy flats, fading in and out. Across the river, on the other side of the Navy yard, the distant rumble of tanks reminded Ethan of the crush of time. His eyes searched the night for something familiar.

Hearing the sound of their car, veterans and sometimes women would pop their heads out of the shacks and tents. They would appear and then retreat, lost in blackness. Ethan knew that tensions were high. People wouldn't trust three unknown men in a car. "It's different at night, Jack. All these shacks look the same," said Ethan. He knew that the Sweeny family was just off the main road. But for this knowledge, they would never find the place. "Stop," he said. "Shut it off. I heard something."

Jack stopped and killed the engine.

"What is it?"

As Ethan listened, a dog barked nearby. Ethan exited the car.

Branko leaped out of the rumble seat and stood next to him. "What is happening?" he asked.

"Shhh..." cautioned Ethan. He listened. "Bosch," he called. "Bosch. Come here." In a few moments, a moving mound of fur jumped into view. The German shepherd was breathing rapidly with excitement. Ethan hugged the dog. "It's Bosch," said Ethan. "They're near here." Bosch smelled both men carefully. Ethan commanded the dog, "home, Bosch, home." The dog looked back and then hopped away. Ethan told Jack, "We're going to follow their dog. He knows the way."

Jack, his hands locked onto the steering wheel, looked mystified. "Hurry," he said.

Zak, still sitting on the bridge railing, watched closely. A truck towed a giant searchlight behind it on the other side of the river. The troops had arrived at the bridgehead, and tanks sat in front of the Navy yard, idling noisily. A small group of cavalrymen on horses took positions on the sides of the road. General MacArthur got out of his staff car. He smoked a cigarette and stood ramrod straight as he talked to his officers. Hundreds of soldiers in full battle dress, armed with rifles and gas grenades, milled about, waiting for orders to move. Zak knew they were coming soon.

A car arrived, and a uniformed man got out and met MacArthur. The two walked up the road away from the others. The new man handed him an envelope. MacArthur appeared to glance at the note and then walked away. The man followed, they talked again, and then he returned to his car and drove away.

MacArthur addressed the group of officers. After a brief discussion, he raised his riding crop and pounded it into his free hand. Within seconds, the officers disbursed and shouted orders to the troops. The searchlight blazed, and its beam was lowered onto the bridge. Zak was blinded by the light. The air was full of the noise of preparation: men barking orders, tank engines revving, excited horses and soldiers moving into position. Zak jumped off the bridge railing and ran. He was joined in retreat by other men standing on the bridge. They knew what was coming. Everyone ran.

Ethan and Branko stumbled through the darkness. They followed the handicapped canine only about thirty feet when they came upon the Sweeny home. "Damn," said Ethan. "It was right here all the time."

"Who's there?" a voice from inside the shack called out.

"Ethan and Branko. Is that you, John?"

A man stepped out carrying an oil lantern. It was John Sweeny. "Ethan. What are you...?"

"John. We came here to get you. You're in great danger. The soldiers are going to attack. You must get your family out of here."

John Sweeny held the light up at shoulder level to make all their faces visible. "Sorry, Ethan. We're not going anywhere. They're not coming into this camp. It would be suicide for them to attack us at night. These men would revolt. Please, Ethan. You shouldn't be here. How did you even get in?"

"We're with Jack Travers. He's in his car over there." Ethan pointed into the blackness. "We're trying to find my sister. She may be here. Have you seen her?"

Just then, Molly Sweeny popped out into the open. "Emma's not with you, is she?"

"No."

"Thank God." Molly put a clenched fist to her mouth.

"She's lost," said Ethan. "She's sick. Very ill. She ran away from the hospital. We thought she would come here." Ethan grabbed Mr. Sweeny by both shoulders and looked directly into his eyes. "John. Save your family before someone gets hurt. Please. Just get in the car, and Jack will drive all of you out of here. Think about the children. Think about Molly."

John Sweeny swallowed and said, "You find your sister, Ethan. I can take care of my family."

Just then, there was the sound of a car horn. The spotlight of Travers' car played across the land and flashed through the maze of junk-filled shanties. In the distance, they heard a shout: "Ethan!" It was Jack calling them. "Ethan. They're coming!"

"Get back in your house," said Ethan. "Branko, please help them."

Branko, Molly, and John Sweeny filed into the shack. Ethan heard the tiny voices of the Sweeny children. They were crying. He ran back to the car. Zak was leaning into the driver's side window listening to Jack. He spotted Ethan, and he signed, *"They're coming. Now! Is Emma here?"*

"No."

"Go back," said Jack. "Get them out! All of them. Take them up the bluffs, away from the camp. Do it now. I'm going to look for Emma." Jack started the engine and pulled away.

Zak and Ethan stood alone in the middle of the road.

"She's not here, Zak. Maybe we were wrong. Maybe the hospital people found her. Jack's right. Come on. We have to get them out."

They dashed back to the Sweeny hut. The searchlight filled the darkness with a blast of white brightness. Screams rode through the night as the people in the camp realized what was happening.

As tear gas canisters exploded near the entrance gate, Zak and Ethan rushed into the house. Molly huddled with the children. Branko shouted at John Sweeny in both English and Serbian, but clearly, there was no time for discussion.

Ethan went outside. The noise from the bridge area was intense, with shouts and screams from people on the run. Then he saw the flames as the soldiers set fire to the tents and shacks. The forced evacuation had started. The firelight revealed another danger. The unmistakable mist of tear gas was in the air.

Ethan ducked into the shelter. "They're burning down the place. And tear gas. We have to run for the bluff!"

The children cried and moaned. Molly stroked Brenda's hair while holding little Colleen in her other arm. Her son, Michael, clung to his mother's arm, staring into her eyes. John Sweeny left the room and went into the tent.

Just then, Ethan was aware of another voice. He turned around and saw his sister standing at the entrance. Emma was covered with dirt. Tears and sweat flowed down her cheeks. Her hair was filled with burrs. He could hardly recognize her. Exhausted, she collapsed onto the floor. Her hand hit the oil lamp as she fell, knocking it over. Oil spilled everywhere and ignited. Flames burst upward, and the cardboard ceiling caught fire. Before the flames reached them, Zak got to Molly and grabbed Michael and Brenda. Effortlessly, he held one toddler under each arm. Molly carried Colleen and rushed out, following Zak. Ethan knelt by Emma's side. In the flickering flames, she looked like she had fallen into hell. Bruised and battered from her two-mile hike through the night, she lay on the canvas tarp gasping for breath. Blood oozed from her mouth. She was dying. Ethan knew she was dying. He grabbed her, lifted her, and cradled her head. The heat was intense. "Emma. Emma. Emma." He called her name, but there was no response.

John Sweeny returned to the burning room. Branko grabbed him. He shouted: "Get out!" Caught in the whirlwind, the roof was sucked up and flew away like a flaming flying carpet, opening the sorry shack to the outside. Bosch, outside the conflagration, barked furiously.

After a few seconds, Molly Sweeny rushed back in, holding her baby on her chest. As she entered, calling out for her husband, she tripped over Ethan and Emma on the floor. Colleen flew out of her hands, landing on the automobile seat they used as a sofa. The baby bounced in the air but survived the fall. She wailed. Somewhere nearby, a soldier was doing his job. Five seconds later, the unmistakable sound of a tear gas canister exploding filled the remains of their shelter. Noxious tear gas mixed with the smoke and flames of the burning shack.

"Get out!" Ethan yelled. As the tear gas filled her lungs, Emma showed signs of life. She coughed and gasped for air. Ethan held her tightly.

The baby coughed, her tiny face red and her eyes full of tears. Molly held her and placed a handkerchief over her baby's face. But Molly was also in a terrible state. Eyes watering, coughing, she yelled for her husband.

Ethan lifted his sister, who was a total dead weight. With great effort, he swung her over his shoulder.

In the dense fog of tear gas, John and Molly stood with their faces illuminated by the flames. They wore looks of horror. Colleen had stopped coughing. Molly shook the baby and shouted her name. John Sweeny looked at his dead daughter. He said one word: "Bastards." Molly cried and brought her baby close to her breast.

John Sweeny ran back into the burning tent. Seconds later, carrying a souvenir from his past, he dashed to the doorway with the explosive grenade in his hand. He was a soldier now, back in the trenches of France, ready to destroy the enemy, possessed by his past.

Carrying Emma over his shoulder, Ethan gathered up Molly. She cradled her lifeless baby, and the four of them escaped. Outside the remains of their shelter, everything was burning. The entire camp was an inferno. Flaming pieces of cardboard flew into his eyes. With his free hand, Ethan covered his mouth. Coughing and hacking, he fought off the tear gas all around him. Something landed on Emma. Her hair started on fire, but Ethan brushed it out immediately. He spun around and saw John Sweeny wrestling with Branko. It looked like the Serbian was trying to take the grenade from him.

Like monsters from Mars, two gas-masked soldiers with rifles and bayonets appeared out of nowhere. One slowed down and glanced at Ethan. He shouted some garbled words that got trapped in his mask and then moved on. Ethan looked at the main road. Structures were aflame on both sides. Soldiers ran about, stopping to toss more gas grenades into the camp. There appeared to be no order or direction. Reckless, wild, and wanton, the soldiers attacked viciously. For the thousands of people in the camp, it was complete panic. Women, men, and children rushed in all directions, trying to flee the flames and the gas. It was a tragic scene of total turmoil.

John Sweeny and Branko still struggled. Branko shouted, "You not do this!" Sweeny pushed Branko to the ground. The veteran stood tall, a silhouette defined by flames and flying embers and the raking path of the searchlight. A squad of soldiers marched toward them double-time on the main road. Arming their gas grenades not forty feet away, they were an easy target for the war veteran. He pulled the pin on the explosive grenade and swung his arm back. But something happened. Maybe sweat filled his hand. Perhaps the tear gas overwhelmed him. The live grenade flew out of Sweeny's hand backward like a wounded duck and landed a few feet from Ethan, hitting softly in the mud.

Still wearing Emma like a shawl, Ethan dove to the ground. As he did, he saw the Serbian rise up, run two steps, and fall upon the deadly device. The explosion ripped through the night. Ethan lay atop his sister, his body pummeled by flying stones and debris. His ears rang. His eyes burned. But, so far as he knew, he was not wounded. He looked at Emma. She was dazed but breathing.

As Branko lay on the ground a few feet away, smoke rose from the Serbian's smoldering body; Ethan reached out and rolled him over. Branko's eyes blinked; incredibly, he was still alive.

"Emma?" The word dripped out of his mouth as a question. Ethan could only read his lips.

"She's OK. She's OK." Branko strained to understand.

Ethan gave him a thumbs-up.

Branko wore a little smile, his head dropped, and his face sunk into the mud.

Ethan tried to digest the catastrophic events. He lay next to his fallen comrade, shocked and deaf to any sound. He rolled his head over to check on Emma, but she was gone. Jack Travers had her now. He was carrying her in his arms. Ethan lifted his head for a better view. Travers slid her through the open door of the roadster onto the front seat. He slammed the door, ran around the car, got in, and drove away.

Ethan's head fell back into the mud. He didn't move a muscle; he didn't think. He couldn't.

-Chapter XX-

Argonne Redux

Zak hustled up the embankment at the south side of Camp Marks. He had carried the two children, Michael and Brenda, under each arm, through the tear gas and flames, through the crush of panicked people, and beyond the lines of soldiers to the bluff's base. While he was breathing hard, his exceptional strength and stamina allowed him to keep going. Amid their escape, Zak had heard an explosion different from the sound of the tear gas canisters. It was a sound that worried him greatly. Molly trailed behind him with baby Colleen nestled in her arm. Bosch, the three-legged dog, kept pace with his master.

They, along with hundreds of others, climbed the hill to safety. Reaching the top, Zak gently laid the Sweeny children down on the soft grass and then looked back to view the destruction. The camp was totally in flames. The tarpaper, canvas, cardboard, and old wood used to build the humble shacks were ideal kindling for the soldier's torches. Tear gas permeated the air, but most remained trapped by the embankment in the valley below. People poured out of the inferno and crawled up the hill. Some tried to carry their meager possessions with them, but as they struggled to be free of the intense heat and caustic fumes, they dropped their things in favor of saving their lives. A pregnant woman ran hand in hand with her children. Some veterans stood tall, shouting orders and guiding people through the smoke toward the hills. Below, a squad of soldiers spotted the survivors on the bluff. They looked directly at Zak's location as if it was their next target of an attack, but their leader called them off, and they continued their east-west sweep, removing stragglers.

Molly struggled to climb the hill. Going to her aid, Zak slid down the slope, using his feet to slow his descent.

Someone was crying. It was the baby. "Zak," she said, smiling. "Colleen is back. Saints alive! It's a miracle. She's all right."

Zak smiled and took the baby from her. He held the little girl firmly but gently, and she stopped crying. He had a way with babies. Together, they climbed the hill. They were greeted by Michael and Brenda at the top.

Brenda cried, Molly hugged her, and the little girl buried her head into her mother's chest. "Where are the others? Where is John? I thought they were right behind us?" asked Molly. Her Irish face glowed yellow-red in the firelight. Tears of joy and fear slid down her cheeks.

Zak shrugged his shoulders, and using hand motions, he indicated he was going back. He slid down the hill and ran toward the flaming maze. Having seen the soldiers use their bayonets to poke and prod, he was careful to dodge around them. The remains of the Sweeny house were unrecognizable. Finally, he spotted John Sweeny, still in the middle of the road, hunched over and hacking, his hands on his knees for support. Zak ran to him. Sweeny's back was turned to him. His tan shirt was pockmarked with small holes, still seeping blood. Zak moved around to face him.

Sweeny looked up. He was a beaten man. Tears filled his eyes. "My little Colleen," he cried. "They've killed her. I've killed her."

Zak tried to make the man understand that the baby was alive. However, he could not communicate. Beyond, Ethan lay on the ground, not moving. Branko lay next to him in the mud. Behind them, the remains of the Sweeny household slowly burned out. He ran to his friend. Ethan recognized him and eased his body up. *"Are you OK?"* asked Zak.

Slowly, Ethan got to a sitting position, raised his hands, and signed. *"Bomb went off. Need to get him to a doctor."* He looked over at Branko.

Zak helped Ethan to his feet. *"I'm going to carry him to*

the bridge. You go up the hill and take Sweeny with you.
Colleen is alive. Tell him that if you can."

Ethan nodded. Zak picked up Branko and slung him
over his shoulder. The Serbian was limp and
unresponsive, and Zak had little hope for the man. Ethan
asked Zak if he could handle it. Zak nodded. Ethan
hobbled toward John Sweeny, guiding him out and Zak
followed behind, carrying the body.

He left Ethan with the wounded war vet and walked
rapidly toward the bridgehead. Branko was a light load
for a "bio-man" like Zak, but it was a painful trek knowing
that his Serbian friend was probably dead. His eyes full
of tears, he surveyed the area. It was as if a meteor had
struck, with complete devastation and destruction. Camp
Marks, and with it the dreams of thousands of veterans,
was dissolving into billowing clouds of smoke, rising into
the air, drifting aimlessly in the darkness over the city of
Washington.

He reached the bridge. The area was a mass of
confusion. Firemen had arrived, and their searchlights
knifed into the darkness; the water from their fire hoses
subdued the raging fires. Soldiers, overwhelmed by their
own devices, masks removed, leaned against the bridge,
gathering their senses. As he approached, a couple of
Army men tried to question him. He looked into the eyes
of these men and sensed their shame. Their heads hung
low. They directed him to the waiting ambulances on the
other side of the bridge.

He kept going. At the head of the bridge, an ambulance
had just arrived, pulling in behind another departing. Zak
stood in front of the vehicle with Branko's body on his
shoulder. His back was wet with sweat and Branko's
blood. He hadn't looked at Branko's stomach wound, but
he knew it was there. He couldn't bear to see the lethal
damage wrought by the grenade.

In less than a minute, the ambulance driver and his
aide removed a stretcher from the back of the wagon and
placed Branko's body onto it. When the driver saw
Branko's wound, the look on his face was telling. With

great care, the two men loaded Branko into the back of the vehicle. Zak stood alone watching the white ambulance drive away, its siren screaming, past the gathering of tanks, horses, and soldiers. He silently mouthed, "Goodbye, Branko, my friend." Then he turned and walked back onto the bridge. Soldiers on either side watched him head back into the melee. They may have ordered him to stop. He kept walking and, with a few steps, disappeared into a wall of smoke and fumes.

He made it back to the bluff. In the blackness of night, he walked slowly and carefully along the elevated, refugee-strewn path, dodging the coughing, vomiting bodies of men, women, and children who lay exhausted on the grass. Eventually, he found the Sweeny family and Ethan. He asked Ethan about Emma and was told that Jack had taken her away in his car. That was all Ethan remembered. Zak wanted to know how Branko had died, but that could wait.

Later that night, the flames died, the soldiers stopped attacking, and some level of sanity returned to the thousands on the hill and those hiding in the nearby fields. Somewhere nearby, a harmonica saved from flames met the parched mouth of a veteran. He blew into the instrument and played "Taps." The solemn music drifted along, riding the same light breeze that had carried the *gaz lacrymogène*, the gas of tears. John Sweeny broke down and cried while his wife and children huddled around him.

Blessed or cursed with an incredible ability to actively sense the emotions of others, Zak was filled with the angst of thousands of beaten, hopeless, and homeless people around him. He pondered the ultimate outcome of the events of this memorable day, July 28, 1932. He wondered if anything had changed as he quietly cried with John Sweeny and his mates.

General Douglas MacArthur had accomplished his mission. The men of the Bonus Expeditionary Force had been expelled. At this moment, across the Anacostia

River, he was being interviewed by reporters. He called the men on the hill "insurrectionists" and claimed that few of the men who came to occupy Washington were actual veterans, Communists, maybe criminals, but not veterans. Speaking of the World War veterans, he said to the gathered newspapermen: "The *mob* down Pennsylvania Avenue looked bad. They were animated by the spirit of revolution. The gentleness and consideration with which they had been treated had been mistaken by them as weakness, and they had come to the conclusion that they were about to take over the government in an arbitrary way or by indirect methods."

LOG of Zak Newman

July 29, 1932 (local time): 8:36 (Day 17 of time travel)

Sleep was impossible, but at least the horrible nightmare was over. This morning, standing on the top of the bluff, my view of the remains of Camp Marks reveals a wasteland. The fires have burned out. Steam rises from pools of muddy water, and burned-out structures smolder. The scene looks like 20th-century photos of the battlegrounds in Europe, gray skies, no trees, no life, the land pockmarked with water-filled shell holes, and the fog of war hanging low. A few soldiers and others who might be government officials are walking around the site, peering into the wreckage as if seeking a clue to the meaning of it all. With the rising sun, the refugees who spent the night on this hill or in the nearby fields have moved on. They have seen the power of their government in action, and they no longer have the will to protest, complain, request, demand, or speak. Their backs have been broken by Hoover, MacArthur, and the Army. Simple men seeking a simple solution to their simple economic problem have been rebuffed by their elected representatives. For them, the system did not work. Somehow now, the beehive of veterans knows where to go next. Most have departed and are heading for a place called Johnstown, Pennsylvania. Few remain.

Ethan and I said our goodbyes to the Sweeny family this morning. John Sweeny appears to be shell-shocked. He didn't say a word this morning. He wore the vacant look of a man lost in time. I don't think he remembers what happened last night. Molly cleaned up his back wounds as best she could. He will need a doctor to remove the pieces of shrapnel. He and his wife are unaware that his actions killed Branko, and we did not tell them. Nothing can be gained now, and much can be lost.

We have no idea of the historical impact of the events of last night. The result of this entire affair appears to be different than our history. No soldiers were killed. No soldiers killed any veterans.

It seems impossible that the violence of yesterday could be ending in a whimper of regret, but that appears to be fact. The marchers have left. The soldiers have left. The Bonus March protest is done. Rocks, bricks, and epitaphs against tanks, sabers, rifles, and noxious gas — the winner is the Army of 1932 — the loser is the Army of 1918. That is certain. Maybe the American people won also. Maybe the presidential election will proceed.

Ethan and I must leave the area. By now, the authorities realize they have a dead man to account for. I am linked to that man. His blood lingers on my clothes. We will sneak back to our apartment to clean up, to rest, and then to find Emma. Jack Travers took her away last night, in the middle of the battle. We have no news about her. His action to get her out of last night's hellhole makes sense. But his apparent lack of concern about Ethan and Branko seems harsh. He made a choice. We trust that he has taken her to safety and medical assistance. We can only hope.

End 07-29-32

-Chapter XXI-

Goodbye

Jack Travers had wheeled out of Camp Marks with Emma, unconscious, who sat next to him. The same sentry recognized his car, noted "Mrs. Roosevelt's niece" passed out in the passenger seat, and allowed them to pass. With its top up, the Buick traveled quickly through the night, away from the snarling noise of the evacuation scene. The car reached an upstream bridge, and they crossed over the river. Not long now, Jack thought. He pushed the Buick to its limits. It roared through the country roads behind Camp Marks, climbing the gently rolling hills. Searchlights weaving a hypnotic pattern in the night sky caught his eye. He looked down the hill toward the riverfront conflagration. The B.E.F. Camp was a flaming crazy quilt. Fires burned high, illuminating the 11th Street drawbridge, the boats in the river, and the Navy yard buildings. It was at once fascinating and terrible.

He wondered about Ethan and Zak. Instinctively, he had decided to get Emma to safety without regard for her brother's and their friends' lives. He would have to live with the consequences of that decision. He looked at Emma. Her breathing was heavily labored, her face blackened, and her clothes disheveled, but she was alive, and he intended to keep her that way.

He drove along Nichols Avenue, straining his eyes to find the hospital entrance. It came up quickly, and he cut the car's wheels onto the winding network of roads. Travers had been here before as part of Mrs. Roosevelt's public relations efforts. He was familiar with the grounds and knew the people who ran the hospital. He gave a wave to the guard at the gatehouse. Travers didn't know or care whether the man recognized him or not, and he continued racing toward the TB complex. The car pulled into the roundabout in front of the admissions wing and came to a noisy halt.

Jack ran inside to secure help, and soon Emma was back in the hospital. The head nurse was most pleased that Travers had returned her patient. He didn't provide details about the evening but simply told them that he found her wandering along the road. He waited. Hours passed. Totally exhausted, he fell into a deep sleep in a waiting room chair. Morning arrived, and someone shook him awake.

"Mr. Travers," said the nurse.

Jack shook out the cobwebs. "Uh. How is she?"

"Better," said the nurse. "She's struggling, but she is conscious."

"I would like to see her. Right now."

The nurse seemed put off by his demand. "You know patient visits are not usually permitted, Mr. Travers, but Dr. Campbell has made an exception for you. You will be required to take a skin test. And your time will be limited."

"That's understood. I'll speak with the doctor later. Thank you."

He followed the nurse through the corridors leading to Emma's room. She mentioned that they had placed Emma in a different room. "No windows," said the nurse. "There will be no unauthorized dismissal this time." Jack nodded knowingly. Arriving at the room, she motioned for him to enter. "You may have a few minutes with her." She turned away and walked down the corridor, her little white nurse's shoes padding silently along the terrazzo floor.

Jack found Emma on the bed, looking small and delicate like an injured bird. Her raven hair billowed on the white pillow, surrounding her pale but beautiful face. At that moment, he remembered how young, sweet, and innocent she was. He stood over her and softly called her name. She opened her eyes. "Emma. My sweet little Emma."

She struggled to speak. The words couldn't make their

way out. Finally, she was able to say, "Jack." But this was followed by a short coughing fit.

"Don't speak, Emma. Just listen. And listen very carefully."

Her eyelids flickered, but her eyes stayed open, fixed on Travers. He bent over and kissed her on the cheek. "You are back in the same hospital. You have tuberculosis, Emma. This is a problem, but I have a solution. However, you must tell no one about this. I will give you something every day that will make you better over time. However, no one else must know. Do you understand?"

She nodded. Travers elevated her head and shoulders off the pillow. Then he pulled out a small container from his pocket and removed a pill. "I'm giving you a pill. Open up." Her mouth accepted the small gift, and he held a glass of water to her lips to complete the communion. "Is it down?"

She nodded weakly.

"Great." He sat in a chair next to the bed and held her hand. They didn't talk again. She fell asleep. The nurse returned, and she walked him back to the lobby.

The next day, after taking the skin test and speaking at length with Dr. Campbell, he returned. Emma now shared a new room with three other young women. The other women cackled when he entered the room, escorted by the nurse. She announced that Mr. Travers would be visiting the new patient from time to time, as he had been authorized by the hospital administration. Travers nodded to the others but went quickly to Emma's bedside. The nurse pulled a curtain between the patients, which provided some level of privacy.

Emma actually greeted him with a small smile. Jack considered that a victory.

"Jack. Where is Ethan? Is he all right? What about Zak?" She was at the limits of her breath already, so she stopped.

Jack pulled his chair closer to the bed. "I see you have

a room with a view again. They must trust you."

She chuckled and coughed.

He reached into his coat pocket and pulled out the little glass pill bottle while she watched. "Do you remember what I told you yesterday?" She nodded. "Good." Today, she was able to bring her body up on her own. Silently, he slipped the pill into her mouth and gave her a drink.

"Ethan?" she asked.

"He's fine, Emma. So is Zak. In fact, they are here today in the lobby, proudly showing off their negative skin tests. But they can't come to see you."

"Why not? I want to see them."

"Hospital rules. It took all my persuasion powers to get permission to be with you." He helped her lie down flat again. "Emma, you will be here for many months. I will always be here for you. Do you understand?" He bent over and whispered in her ear. "I love you, Emma. You don't have to worry. Everything will be fine."

Emma looked up at the ceiling, then back to Jack. "Everything is happening so fast, Jack. But I have to get back home. What day is it?"

"It's Saturday."

"What's the date?"

Jack thought for a moment. "It's the 30th of July."

"You have to get me out of here, Jack."

"Did you hear what I just said? I will take care of you." He leaned in and kissed her on the cheek.

She smiled a tiny smile. She spoke softly, "I love you, too, Jack. With all my heart. But I cannot stay. I can't."

Travers leaned back and smiled. "That's music to my ears. You don't understand, my dear. You're required to be here until you are well. You can't go anywhere for many months. These folks consider you and your illness a little dangerous to the public. Anyway, by that time, I would hope that you wouldn't want to leave. That you would want to be with me at your side."

"But what about my brother?"

"He and Zak understand completely. You must stay

here to get well. That's just the way it is. They get it." Jack leaned back in his chair. "They are going home for a while. They'll tell your father what happened. Maybe he can come down and visit later when you get better. Then we can have a big party to celebrate."

"And Branko..."

Jack glanced up at the ceiling. "Branko is gone. He had to leave. He wanted me to say goodbye. He said that you would always be in his heart."

"He is such a nice man," she said.

Jack pondered the lie. However, they had all agreed it would be best if they didn't tell her now.

Emma said nothing. She was obviously thinking. "Can I just see them once before they go?"

Jack smiled. "Your brother and Zak?"

She nodded. "It's imperative, Jack."

"Well, I'll try, Emma. But this place is like a prison. They've got rules. But let me see." He stood up and pulled the pill bottle out again. He held it in front of him.

She looked at it.

"Remember. Mum's the word."

"I understand, Jack."

He leaned over and kissed her. She reached out and hugged him.

"Don't leave me, Jack."

"Don't be silly. Like the song says, I need 'someone to watch over me.'"

She smiled. "Me too."

Three men stood on a slight rise overlooking a green expanse dotted with headstones. A few mountains as a backdrop, and Branko might have thought of this place as home; it was going to be his permanent residence. Ethan, Zak, and Jack stood next to the open grave. Branko's casket had already been lowered into place. In the background, two gravediggers sat on a large rock waiting patiently, smoking cigarettes, and conversing quietly. Jack looked at Ethan. "You want to say a few words?"

Ethan nodded. Still subject to the hay fever that seemed to flare up outdoors, he wiped his nose with a handkerchief and dried the tears in his eyes with the same cloth. After thinking for a moment, Ethan began, "We hardly knew our friend Branko. But we knew what kind of man he was. He was a brave and thoughtful immigrant. Like many of us, a strange traveler in a strange world. He saved my sister's life twice...and my own life. I know he wanted to make the world a better place. I think he saw too much bloodshed and grief in the war. He came here to start a new life, but that dream has ended. We owe him our lives, and we owe him our eternal gratitude. I can't be certain, but I think he is, at this moment, the most important man in America. No matter...we send this man, Gvozden Brkovic, whom we know as Branko, to the top of the big top...may he fly forever in all our hearts."

They dropped their heads for a moment of silence. Then, each tossed a handful of dirt onto the casket. Travers watched his dirt fall and splatter on the wooden box below. He knew this would be the end of Branko in more ways than one. His grave would remain unmarked. It was bought and paid for by the Bureau of Investigation. Travers suspected they had used him in some capacity; otherwise, they wouldn't have an interest in the former circus performer from Serbia. There was no mention of his activities in Camp Marks on the night that ended his life. Hoover, with spies everywhere, must have found out about his death and taken custody of his body. Only Travers received notice of his burial.

Any records of Branko's relationship with the government would be as buried as he was, thus saving Mr. Hoover and his bureau any embarrassing publicity. Maybe Hoover thought he was a grenade-toting anarchist or Communist. It was best for the government to bury him and his history, with no mention of any connection to J. Edgar Hoover or his minions.

In silence, they walked back to Jack's car. Jack and Ethan rode in front, with Zak taking his usual post in the

back. Slowly, Jack drove out of the cemetery, knowing he
had turned the page on that bit of history, and he
wondered what future lay ahead for him. He thought
about Emma. Every day she was getting better. Every day
he visited her and gave her the medicine. Each day that
passed brought them closer together. As she improved,
she seemed to be adjusting to the idea of living in his
world.

Overall, things were moving in the right direction.
President Hoover had suffered a political black eye that
he might wear forever. He and General MacArthur
continued to tap dance for the press, but the public was
not enjoying their act. Movie theaters across the country
showed newsreels of the Bonus March carnage. The
images of tanks, poison gas, and cavalry soldiers
swinging sabers at American citizens were inescapably
horrific to a people suffering through the Great
Depression. A photo of the Capitol Building rising above
the flames engulfing the Hooverville shanties stuck in
everyone's mind. It all worked in Franklin Roosevelt's
favor. Again, his political instincts were correct. He didn't
have to do anything. President Hoover dug his own
political grave. It was reported that Jack's boss, upon
reading news stories of the events, asked, "Why didn't
Hoover offer the men coffee and sandwiches instead of
turning Doug MacArthur loose?"

On the road leading back to the city, Jack glanced at
Ethan. "So you'll be leaving soon?"

"Yes, I'm afraid so. I hate to leave Emma."

"The good news is that she's getting better. Don't
worry. I'll take good care of her," said Travers.

"I'm sure you will, Jack. But...we have been together
since birth. We're twins, you know. We've never been
apart."

"Everything is subject to change, Ethan. Things are
not necessarily as they might seem to be. Maybe all of this
is for the best...only time will tell."

Ethan watched the countryside slowly turning into
town. "You're right, Jack. Time will tell."

-Chapter XXII-

Flying to the Future

The time travelers were running out of time. They had four days to get back to 2032. Ethan accepted that Emma would have to remain in 1932. As Zak said, "Who can plan a hundred years behind?" Jack had worked his magic. He had secured the hospital's permission for a brief farewell for Emma with her brother and Zak. Jack had also agreed to sit this one out in the hospital lobby while they waited on the outdoor balcony, nervously anticipating her arrival.

The second-floor view on this clear summer morning was exceptional. Ethan and Zak sat on the low balcony wall and surveyed the lush green countryside, pouring into the valley, converging on the other side of the river to meet the city of Washington. From this distant vantage point, there was no evidence of the previous week's death and destruction. Washington, D.C., had returned to its August norm: hot, sleepy, and peaceful.

"Looks quiet down there, doesn't it?" signed Zak.

"Very nice. Life goes on."

"And no martial law."

Ethan laughed. "I'm looking forward to the election results, which should be available in the new, revised *History* when we get back. That should be fun reading."

"We'll see. You never know what will happen when you jump into the past."

"Have faith, Zakaroo. I think we did it."

"Emma will be excited to hear."

"I'm sure she will. You know, I talked to her doctor, and he said her recovery, so far, is remarkable...."

The door opened loudly, and Emma, seated in a wheelchair, rolled onto the balcony. She was all smiles. The nurse parked her in front of Ethan and Zak.

"Fifteen minutes, gentlemen," said the woman in white.

"Got it," said Ethan. "Thanks."

The nurse departed into the building. Ethan hugged his sister. Then Zak joined in for a group hug. Tears filled Emma's eyes.

"I am so happy to see you. I missed you both," said Emma, drying her tears with a handkerchief.

"Me too, Sis."

"Ethan..." she said with a pained look on her face.

"Sorry. Just testing your state of mind."

"My mind's as sharp as ever, brother dear. I'm feeling better every day. I can't see why they won't let me leave with you."

"It's a process, Emma. It's 1932. Things take time. Just be glad that you made it through. The last time we saw you, you looked pretty shaky."

"What? You didn't like my grand entrance? It was just like the movies."

"Right," said Ethan. "Very exciting."

"Was anyone hurt? Is the Sweeny family OK? And Branko? And you guys?"

"Everyone is fine, Emma. Whatever happens, the future will be better for everyone. Our little venture was a big success."

"No nationwide riots?"

"Nope. Nothing but a whole lot of pissed-off voters. It's looking good for our guy."

Emma smiled. "That is good news. I feel better now. Heck, I'll even be here to watch it all unfold. I'll be part of your history."

"*Maybe you can vote for Franklin Roosevelt in three months,*" signed Zak.

"I don't think I'll push the envelope. I'm just going to get well and enjoy the ride."

"*With Jack?*" asked Zak, wearing an unmistakable twinkle in his eye.

"Oh, Zak. Are you jealous?"

Zak didn't answer. He just made a face and nodded.

"Come here, you," she said.

He knelt down, and she grabbed him by his shoulders, pulled him into her, and kissed him solidly on the lips, holding it for several seconds.

"Hey, kids," said Ethan. "You're spreading germs."

"*Vete a la fregada,*" said Zak as he pulled away. He blushed. "*Let me savor the moment.*"

"OK. Loverboy."

"You're next, Ethan."

He bent over, and she kissed him on top of his head.

"I am honored, m'lady," said Ethan, backing away as if he had just been knighted by the queen.

They chatted aimlessly for a few more minutes, happy to be alive and together. Then the nurse returned. She stood before them and glanced at her watch. "Time's up. Mr. Travers is waiting for you."

Both Ethan and Zak put forth one last hug. Emma began to tear up again.

"See you in a few months," she said.

"Right. See you then. Get healthy, and be good," said Ethan.

"Tell Dad that I love him."

Ethan swallowed hard. "I will, Emma, I will." He and Zak turned and walked away quickly to avoid getting caught up in the moment.

They looked back and waved goodbye.

Emma smiled. "Have a safe trip home. I love you both."

They rode with Jack. He drove straight from St. Elizabeth's Hospital to the airport. At about 10:30, the car pulled into Washington-Hoover Airport on the west side of the Potomac River near Arlington National Cemetery. Ethan and Zak were impressed with the new sparkling white Art Deco terminal building. Everything was done on a miniature scale. The terminal was two stories high, with rooftop viewing platforms on both wings of the building and a lounge in the center. It looked like something from a vintage toy train set. 1932 air travel was uncomplicated, thought Ethan. Travers parked the car directly in front. It was the only car in the lot. They removed their bags from the Buick and came to the driver's side.

"Well, Jack. Appreciate everything you have done for us. And for Emma," said Ethan.

"It was quite an experience. Added a lot of excitement to my job. Are you sure you have enough funds to get home?"

"Not a problem. We've got fifty-four bucks for our tickets to Boston via Newark and plenty enough for a train trip home."

"Did you call your father to tell him that you were returning?"

"Yes. He's upset about Emma, but he understands. He'll be waiting for us at the train station."

"Good. See you in a few months, then." Jack eyed the two men carefully.

Ethan looked at him directly. "We'll be back. We promised Emma that we'll write to her often. We'll keep her informed. Until we get settled, if you need to, you can write to me in care of 'General Delivery' at the Portsmouth, New Hampshire, post office. OK?"

"Right," said Jack. He looked at his watch. "You better get going. Your plane's leaving soon."

"Not to worry. We have reservations. So long, Jack."

Jack threw out handshakes to both Ethan and Zak. "Until we meet again." He waved, slipped the car in gear, and drove off, leaving the time travelers standing alone before the terminal entrance.

"*Portsmouth?*" signed Zak.

Ethan shrugged his shoulders. "Hey, that's our cover, as we agreed. At least it's on the way to Mystic Heights. We'll find someone to send out letters to Emma on a regular basis...I hope."

They grabbed their bags, entered the little terminal, verified their flight, and gazed out the vast windows overlooking the field.

"*Here she comes, Ethan. Ford Tri-Motor, the miracle of flight. We're in business now,*" signed Zak.

Ethan gazed at the small single-wing plane banking

over the amusement park near the river, swinging in for a landing on the tiny field. "This looks like fun. All we have to do is avoid the radio towers and the roller coasters on the way out, and we'll be in good shape."

They boarded the ten-passenger airplane and took their seats. There were only two other passengers on the plane: well-dressed gentlemen who looked like successful businessmen flying to an important meeting. The Depression made travel too expensive for most people, thought Ethan, particularly air travel. He was grateful they brought sufficient funds to pay for this aerial adventure. The pilot fired up the engines. Loud and full of vibration, they surprised Ethan with their ferocity. In a few minutes, the plane was airborne high above Washington.

The time travelers gawked out the window as if they had never traveled by airplane before, which was a fact. Below, streetcars and autos scurried around the city. The plane circled to the left, and they flew over the Saint Elizabeth's Hospital complex, which looked even more impressive from the air. Ethan thought about his sister sitting on the balcony, looking up and seeing their plane. He wished the pilot could waggle his wings for Emma, but he settled for a little wave out his window. "Bye, Emma," he said to himself. The plane flew over the Anacostia, and they viewed the burned-out field of dreams previously called Camp Marks. Everything looked clean, neat, and mundane from their lofty perch, but the time travelers knew that the flat, marshy spot of land below was a hallowed battleground. They spotted the White House, the Capitol dome, and the nearby structures that once housed veterans and Communists. Those buildings were being knocked to the ground by wrecking ball cranes. Soon there would be new government buildings, and Camp Glassford would be forgotten in history.

Zak signed: "*Ninety miles an hour.*"

Ethan laughed. "Incredible. I almost feel faint."

The hour-and-a-half flight went quickly. Ethan busied himself writing letters to Emma. He wrote six in all. When he was done, he commented to Zak. "I fancy myself quite the creative writer. You wouldn't believe what we will be doing in Portsmouth over the next six months."

Zak read through them and laughed. *"That Portsmouth sounds like a fun place,"* he signed.

"We'll find out. We're going to stop there on the way to Mystic Heights. Maybe I'll buy you a burger and fries."

"You're on, Mr. Wright, with a chocolate shake chaser."

After landing in Newark, they switched planes. By 3 o'clock, they were in Boston. From there, they rode a train north to Portsmouth, New Hampshire, a place they had never been before, in any year. It proved to be an interesting place, full of history, but the time travelers were running out of time. This was day twenty-four. They decided to get a hotel room, stay the night, and leave for Mystic Heights in the morning. They ate well at the hotel. Zak dispensed with the burger idea, which surprisingly was not on the menu. Instead, they had a delightful multi-course meal that included freshly caught fish, homemade bread, and locally brewed beer. All this excellent food caused Ethan to wonder and prompted him to ask, "What do you think we are eating when we eat food at home, Zak? It's certainly not real food like this."

"Don't even think about it, Ethan. Just enjoy the meal," Zak signed.

The next day, they tested the waters with the hotel's bell captain. Ethan came up with a semi-plausible story about his sick sister in Washington: Zak and he would soon be traveling to China, and therefore would the bell captain kindly mail these stamped letters, one each month, starting next month. A five-dollar bill from Ethan cemented the deal. The bell captain swore he would faithfully send the letters. With that out of the way, they left the hotel and went to the post office to find out what would happen to "General Delivery" mail that was not picked up. They were told such mail was held for a year and then burned. That was fine with them. Emma, who was in on the game, would mail a return letter from the hospital after receiving one from Ethan. Thus, if anyone inquired, it would appear that she and Ethan were communicating.

Mid-morning, Ethan and Zak sat comfortably in the coach car of a half-empty train headed for Mystic Heights. They had enough time to travel back to their hometown, climb up to the top of the rocky cliff overlooking Smuggler's Cove, and get into position for their time-travel return to the year 2032. They didn't know what would happen if they exceeded Dr. Currant's twenty-eight-day timetable for return, and they didn't want to find out.

"This sure beats freight-hopping," signed Zak. Ethan, reading a newspaper, didn't respond, so Zak tapped him on the shoulder and repeated his comment.

"Always better to ride in a train rather than under it or in a boxcar," said Ethan. He held the paper high to read something. "Did you know they discovered the positron a couple of days ago?"

"What's a positron?"

"I don't know, but it says it's the antiparticle of an electron. Hard to believe we can operate Dr. Currant's machine so well when we know so little about the world of physics," commented Ethan.

"It's like driving an automobile. Once you do it, you never forget."

"I hope so. We'll find out soon. So far, everything is going smoothly. Hey, here's an article about the evacuation. President Hoover is quoted as saying, 'A challenger to the authority of the United States Government has been met, swiftly and firmly.' I have to agree with him on that. Maybe I'd add the word 'brutally.'"

"Anything on Mr. Roosevelt?"

"Yep. They have Franklin Roosevelt's acceptance speech at the Democratic Convention last month." He found the page. "I'll read you part of it. This is pretty good stuff. 'Never before in modern history have the essential differences between the two major American parties stood out in such striking contrast as they do today. Republican leaders not only have failed in material things, they have failed in national vision because in disaster, they have held out no hope; they have pointed out no path for the people below to climb back to places of security and of safety in our American life.' And I like this one, 'This is more than a political campaign; it is a call to arms.'"

"He was right on. It was a 'call to arms.' Hoover took him up on that. But I think old Herbie is losing the war now."

"Thanks to Branko," said Ethan.

"Hombre valiente..."

"Mucho valiente." Ethan gave Zak a thumbs-up. "And you too, my friend. We did it."

Zak returned the thumbs-up.

Ethan nodded. "I'm guessing General MacArthur and his army will be looking for another enemy to fight. Somebody other than the American people."

"We can only hope."

-Chapter XXIII-

No Cigar

When their train pulled in at about 4:15 that afternoon, the Mystic Heights railroad station was an anthill of action. The time travelers jumped from the train onto the platform, excited to be home. The churning steam locomotive echoed in the background while porters with baggage carts milled about energetically. People would not notice strangers arriving on a train. It was a college town, so the permanent residents were accustomed to the comings and goings of young men like Ethan and Zak. A hundred years from now, both of them had attended Cordwell University. Comfortable in the setting, they moved nonchalantly out the front door. They ignored the ancient black-and-white taxis standing in a row. They would walk to their final destination because they needed to stretch their legs, and they wanted their short trip to the top of the cliff overlooking the bay to be a private undertaking.

Main Street in Mystic Heights was lined with shops on the landside and a boardwalk on the waterside. The two future residents walked along the promenade. The adjacent beach was filled with people enjoying the best of the short summer season. It was a windy day, with swimmers bobbing in the water, fighting the surf, and soaking up the late afternoon sun.

"*We should go for a swim,*" signed Zak.

"Right," said Ethan. "Let's make some new friends while we're here. Maybe we'll run into their great-grandchildren later in the day."

"*OK, Boss. Onward and upward.*"

They ambled along the beach, heading for the winding gravel road that began beyond Main Street's bend. They had slightly less than an hour to get there and set up to jump into the future. The *TimeTravelle* would cycle at 6 o'clock.

"Hope we don't find any picnickers on top of the cliff. We don't need any witnesses to our disappearing act," said Ethan.

Zak wasn't paying attention. He was watching the young women in swimsuits sunning themselves on the beach.

"Hey, Zakaroo, I know you can't talk now, but can you walk, look, and hear at the same time?"

Zak looked up at Ethan. *"The girls are checking us out, man."*

"Right, and maybe they'd like to come back with us to 2032."

"Hey, we could even stay here overnight. We've got plenty of time."

"Forget it, Romeo. Focus on getting back. Got it?"

Zak nodded and then looked back to catch another glimpse of the girls. He waved at them, and they smiled and waved back. *"We should try to have more fun on these trips. All work and no play makes Zak a dull boy."*

"Save your energy for later, when we deal with Dr. Currant. He's going to be pissed."

Zak contemplated meeting with Dr. Currant and Ethan's father coming soon. It was bad enough that they would have to deal with the expected consequences of illicitly commandeering the *TimeTravelle*, but they would also have to explain why Emma wasn't with them. He didn't look forward to that conversation. The boardwalk ended. They followed a sandy beachfront footpath lined on both sides with tall grass. After a five-minute trek, they arrived at the road leading up the hill, set down their bags, and rested. Zak looked over his shoulder. No one was following them.

"Coast is clear. Vamos a Chihuahua?"

"Bow-wow," said Ethan.

They grabbed the bags and started climbing up the road that would become Memorial Drive many years in the future. However, at this time, it was just potholed hardscrabble, hardly satisfactory for foot traffic, and definitely unsuitable for automobiles. Ten minutes later, they arrived at the top of the hill, somewhat out of breath but relieved to have reached their destination. They were above the cliff. Far below, the blue waters of the bay rippled with wave action. A steady wind blew across the rocky ground into their faces.

"Nobody here," said Ethan. "Let's get set up."

They looked for the pile of fallen branches that they had used to conceal the markers of their jump landing locations. Only a few weeks had passed, but everything had changed. Fierce storm winds must have blown away the branches. There was no evidence of a pile. They walked around the rocky top, trying to get their bearings.

"Damn," said Ethan. "I know it was around here someplace." He looked up the hill to his right and exclaimed, "Wait, isn't that our rock?" They walked quickly to the small boulder. "Hey. This is it. At least the wind didn't blow this around. How about our other markers?"

Zak remembered that they had placed the boulder in the center of the landing area. Someplace at the outer edge, maybe twenty feet from the rock, they should find their landing points that they had marked with stones. There should be three groupings. They wandered about the perimeter carefully, trying to avoid disturbing anything. It was too late. Something or somebody had moved their markers. *"Where are the stones, Ethan?"* asked Zak.

"I hate to say it, but I think these are them." He pointed with his foot to a scattering of small rocks. "Sure, here's some more. It's about the right spot." He walked around in a large circle. "And here's Emma's spot. She faces the water, and I'm directly opposite. You should have your back to the town. There are only a few loose rocks here. The wind couldn't have done it. Maybe some animal."

"Right, a rock hound?"

"I don't know. Maybe kids. Maybe the branches knocked the rocks around when the wind-tossed them everywhere. I don't know. But the good news is that we can figure out roughly where we stood."

"*Roughly?*" That didn't sound like the start of a good time-travel flight.

Ethan ignored his comment. "We're running out of time." He looked around. "There's nobody here but us. Put on your goggles. Get into the center of your rocks. I think we will be very close to our jump points." He wiped his dripping nose one last time. "At least in a few minutes, I'll get rid of this stupid hay fever."

They moved to their landing locations, adjusting in tandem, with Ethan's repositioning resulting in Zak's repositioning, and so on. This little dance went on for several minutes.

"OK. You got it?" asked Ethan.

Zak shrugged his shoulders. He reached into his bag, put on his goggles, and prepared himself for the future, whatever that would be. They were amateurs in the time-travel game. It would be nice to have Dr. Currant here at this moment. He also thought about Emma. Maybe she's the lucky one, all tucked into her hospital bed in Washington with her new boyfriend at her side. What the heck? 1932 was not so bad. In time, she might grow to love it. The wind whistled across his ears and brought up bits of sand and dirt. He looked over at Ethan, who was adjusting his goggles. He had positioned his bag between his feet, just as Zak had done with his. Zak crossed his fingers and gave a game smile to Ethan.

"See you on the other side," said Ethan.

Time passed, maybe a minute or two, then Zak heard the bell ringing in Randall Tower far below, at the edge of the town. It banged out the hours; this was it. He counted: one, two, three, four, five. He heard the sound of the sixth bell very faintly. The swooshing sounds returned, the blackness, the parade of fleeting images in the time tunnel, the white dot in the center of his vision sucking up all his senses like a psychic sponge. Whatever was happening, he disappeared. Whoever he was disappeared. Then the white dot exploded into a burst of blindness.

When he felt his feet hit solid ground, he knew it was over. They had made it. He steadied himself. But the landing bothered him. His skin tingled, and he shivered involuntarily. Why was he so cold? What was hitting him in the face, soft and wet and cold? His vision returned slowly. His entire body shook involuntarily like a dog coming out of a bathtub. Ethan should be right over there, he thought. He looked to his right, and Ethan was visible through a flurry of snowflakes. But it's the middle of summer. He shivered again as much from fear as from the cold.

"Zak?" He heard Ethan's voice.

Ethan removed his goggles and slowly walked toward him. Zak looked around. Nothing was around them, just a barren landscape covered with drifting snow. No laboratory, no town, no seaside, only a grim, desolate, cold bleakness covered in a steel-gray sky. Sprites of snow swirled around them like angry white wasps.

"Zak. I think we made it!" said Ethan. "This must be near the bunker."

Zak could see his own breath billowing out of his mouth. It's winter. It's snowing. He removed his goggles. The little snow pellets stung his eyes. It's all screwed up, he thought. We're screwed.

"We've got to be close, Zak," said Ethan, his voice less than convincing and half blown away by the relentless winds.

Zak looked at him as a doctor would look at a dying patient. "*Maybe close...but no cigar,*" he signed. "*Definitely no cigar.*"

—THE END—

TIME TRAVEL TWINS

W. Green

SAVING JFK
Volume 1

The Twins attempt to stop the Chicago

assassination of JFK in November 1963,

and create a better future for

their world of 2028.

X-OOMING FDR
Volumes 2, 3 4

Determined to redesign history, and the

life of a man who is only a footnote in the

history books of the 21st century, the Twins

travel into danger and intrigue.

SAVING TRUMP
Volume 5

The year is 2016, and the Twins and Zak

team up with their descendants, Samantha and

Jason Keene, during the presidential election.

Donald Trump is in…but does he continue?

BOOKS BY OTHERS RELATED TO THE
EVENTS DESCRIBED IN *X-ooming FDR*

The Bonus Army: An American Epic by Paul Dickson
and Thomas B. Allen.
Published by Walker & Company, 2004.

War is a Racket by Major General Smedley Butler.
Published by World Classics Books, 2010.

Since Yesterday: 1929-1939 by Frederick Lewis Allen.
Published by Bantam Books, 1961.

B. E. F.: The Whole Story Of The Bonus Army by W.W.
Waters and William C. White. Published by Cincinnatus
Press, 2007.

The Last of the Doughboys: The Forgotten Generation
and Their Forgotten World War by Richard Rubin.
Published by Houghton Mifflin Harcourt, 2013.

The Five Weeks of Giuseppe Zangara: The Man Who
Would Assassinate FDR by Blaise Picchi. Published by
Academy Chicago Publishers, 1998.

The Outfit: The Role of Chicago's Underworld in the
Shaping of Modern America by Gus Russo. Published by
Bloomsbury, 2001.

Since Yesterday: 1929-1939 by Frederick Lewis Allen.
Published by Bantam Books, 1965.

The Plots Against the President by Sally Denton.
Published by Bloomsbury Press, 2012.

The Chicago Outfit by John J. Binder. Published by
Arcadia Publishing, 2003.

When Capone's Mob Murdered Roger Touhy by John W. Tuohy. Published by Barricade Books Inc., 2001.

Florida in the Great Depression by Nick Wynne & Joseph Knetsch. Published by The History Press, 2012,

The Plot to Seize the White House by Jules Archer. Published by Skyhorse Publishing, 2007.

It Can't Happen Here by Sinclair Lewis. Published by New America Library, 2005.

FDR's Deadly Secret by Steven Lomazow, M.D. and Eric Fettmann, Public Affairs, 2009.

Devil Dog: The Amazing True Story of the Man Who Saved America by David Talbot with Illustrations by Spain Rodriguez. Published by Simon & Schuster, 2010.

Thanks for Reading

X-ooming FDR 1932

Did you like the book? Your on-line book review will really help the author get the word out.